The Traveler

***

The Hideaway Series

Book 2

By: Mary Theriot

Dedication

Without the love and support of my family and friends, I would not have pursued this new path in life. I would especially like to thank those that have proofread copy after copy, to give me their honest opinion of the books.

To my daughter Theresa, thank you so much for your continued encouragement.

To my wonderful husband Malwen, your continued love and support mean the world to me. I don't know what I would do without you in my life. All of my books wouldn't be what they are, without you pushing me forward.

To my fans, I would like to offer a special thank you for your continued support.

Copyright © 2012 by Mary Reason Theriot
ISBN-10: 1-945393-52-1
ISBN-13: 978-1-945393-52-5

Also Available by Mary Reason Theriot:
The Hunter
The Traveler
Dr. Frankenstein
Above Suspicion
Horror In The Night
Deadly Seduction
Echoes On The Bayou
Seven Deadly Sins
A Kiss So Deadly
A Deadly Combination
CarnEvil of Souls
Seduced by Voodoo
Haunted Visions
Unrequited Love

www.maryreasontheriot.com

Prologue

Motor homes make great vacation vehicles. People travel across the country with the conveniences of home at their fingertips, never worrying with a hotel. However, The Traveler transformed his into something that allowed him the opportunity to commit murder anywhere he liked. His unique vehicle gave a whole new meaning to toy hauler. It had become a portable torture chamber.

His first kill had been unintentional and impetuous; a fortuitous accident that had revealed his course in life. Over the years, he perfected his skill, learning to be innovative with his techniques. He became superb at it, especially since he had no empathy towards people.

The Traveler enjoyed the open road; wandering from town to town, enjoying a gypsy lifestyle. He never stayed in one place long and worked odd jobs here and there when he needed money. The need to accumulate wealth never interested him; he never desired material things. When it came time to leave, he merely drove off into the sunset with no worries. Best of all, by the time someone discovered the body, he was long gone.

At one time, rest stops had been the perfect hunting ground, and a convenient place to dispose of the bodies. Now he had to be careful since most had installed video surveillance and some had twenty-four hour security guards. This forced him to prey on prostitutes, homeless, and runaways; what law enforcement agencies considered high risk victims. But, they didn't give him the same release. Whatever tortures he did, they seemed to accept as their fate. He preferred those that had a good life, who never believed something bad could happen to them. It gave him a thrill when they pleaded for their lives and showed emotion while being tortured. Watching as the life drained from their eyes brought him the rush he sought. With the prostitutes, he was denied that rush.

Over the years, The Traveler became aware of the various stages associated with torturing someone to death. The first stage was fear, which could be seen in the victim's eyes. Next came defiance, when they attempted to fight the inevitable. Then despair, this one brought him such jubilance, when the victim realized he held their fate in his hands and there was no chance of escape. Once the victim realized there was no hope of survival, the next stage began - they pleaded for death to end their suffering. Of course, his revered stage was the last - death.

The Traveler pulled into a truck stop to grab a quick bite to eat. While waiting for his food, a news story piqued his interest, regarding a little town named Hope, Louisiana.

When he heard that David Thorguson would be transferred from the small jail in Hope to Springport Prison in two days, a dangerous plan began to take form. It could be risky to bring in a partner. However, a playmate would make the game he had in mind more interesting.

Chapter 1

The Traveler researched which route the transport van would most likely take. It would be such a pleasure to share his accomplishments with someone who would appreciate his handiwork. Plus, once freed, David Thorguson would be forever in The Traveler's debt. Finally, someone would look up at him with awe, and not down on him with disdain.

The Traveler grew up in the backwoods of West Virginia, where his childhood had been one big nightmare. His dad did everything he could to make ends meet for his family, including working several jobs. Even with that, there never seemed to be enough money. Of course, it didn't help that his dad drank most of it away on Friday nights. His mom tried her hardest to keep her children clothed and fed. But with barely enough money to scrape by, the hateful kids at school constantly bullied and teased him about his pieced together clothes and his shoes that were held together with glue and tape. The Traveler dreamed of ways his tormentors should pay for their cruelty. They probably still lived in the lap of luxury, harassing and humiliating those they could. Their offspring may even be the same way. Perhaps with David's help, he could hand out some much needed justice. He wanted to make the people of Lake Hamilton pay, and David would know how to accomplish this. After all, he terrorized Hope for months and eluded capture.

***

He popped the hood to the RV. Feigning a broken down vehicle was easier than attempting a rear end accident. He didn't want to draw attention, and damage to either vehicle could do just that. By the time Springport Prison realized their prisoner hadn't arrived, they would have a few hours head start.

While waiting, he watched as the oppressive heat radiated from the blacktop in shimmering waves. The Traveler missed the cooler weather of the northern states. If not for David, he would have avoided Louisiana altogether. He was on a mission though, one that made this inconvenience worthwhile.

The Traveler stepped out onto the road, with his arms waving, when he saw the approaching prison van. This forced the guard to stop for him - it was either stop or hit a pedestrian.

"Thank you for stopping. I was beginning to wonder how long I would be out here. My RV broke down, and there is no signal for my cell at all."

"I'm sorry, but the only assistance I can provide is to radio in ..."

The guard never completed his sentence. Quickly reaching behind his back for his Taser gun, he subdued the guard. He gathered the unconscious man and brought him into the special room in the RV. Once he undressed the guard; he restrained him as a present for his guest.

***

Deputy Rick Olivier found himself in a predicament when he came to. The last thing he remembered was stopping to help a man on the side of the road. If he managed to get out of this mess, the warden would chew his ass.

He knew the prison would conduct an all-out manhunt when he didn't show up. But what was the reasoning behind this? Who would want to set David Thorguson free? Hopefully someone in Hope would notice something amiss and not hand the prisoner over to the imposter.

He had drawn the short straw when it came to this pick up. He was biding his time with this job for an opening at the state trooper's academy. But until then, bills had to be paid. Since his wife, Debbie, was due any day now with their first child, he also needed the insurance. He never considered something like this happening.

As he tried to free his hands, he realized that the handcuffs were too tight. A shiver of fear ran through his body when he thought about the things that could happen to him.

Chapter 2

The Traveler didn't have much time to convince David he was here to help him as he pulled the transport van off the road. He hoped that by giving David the guard, he would realize he was here to free David from the hell he had been forced to live this past year.

After ensuring the van was hidden from the road, he stepped out of the vehicle and unlocked the door. "Relax my friend, I am here to help you, but we have to hurry. I want to be well on our way before anyone realizes that you have escaped."

As he removed the shackles from David's wrists, he continued to explain. "I am a fellow brother, and I am here to help you but we must hurry. My RV is hidden behind the van. To show you my support I have a gift for you. But again, I must stress that we hurry."

When David went to lurch for him, The Traveler quickly pulled out the knife he had kept tucked in the back of his waistband. "I don't want to hurt you, but we must leave quickly. I will explain everything while we are on the road." Smiling, he continued to explain, "You must have certain hungers which need to be met, and I hope what I have waiting will curb your appetite."

David's curiosity must have gotten the better of him, because he visibly relaxed and followed The Traveler out of the van.

The Traveler quickly unlocked the RV's side door, and ushered David inside. "Come inside and let me show you what I have for you."

He could feel David as he peered over his shoulder as he opened the hidden door. "I know you prefer women, but he should help satisfy your appetite for now."

At the sight of the two men, the guard began fighting against his restraints. "Once we are on the road, you are more than welcome to quench any desires you may have, but I do believe we should become better acquainted first."

One look at David and The Traveler knew he was anxious to kill. He had that look in his eyes - one of a predator. A man with no pity, remorse, or compassion for others. Yes, David may indeed be just like him.

Closing the bedroom door, The Traveler stated, "He will be fine back here for now. Let's get this journey started and leave Louisiana quickly my friend."
Holding out his hand, he introduced himself, "I am called The Traveler."

"It's nice to meet you, *mon ami*. I'm still unsure why you helped me escape, though."

As they fastened their seatbelts, The Traveler laughingly stated. "Let's just say that we are kindred spirits."

The Traveler watched as David scrutinized him. "I take it you aren't a cop then?" David asked.

"No, I am not a cop."

"So, who are you?"

"I am but a simple traveler who enjoys the countryside and the people associated with it." Glancing over at David as he eased the RV onto the road he added, "As I said, I am the same as you."

"Same as me, huh?"

"Well, actually I may be a little wiser than you in some ways. I prefer to keep my talents hidden."

David nodded as he looked around. "Hmmm. Well, just what is it that you do?"

"For work, I take an odd job here and there when I need money. Most of the time I simply take money from my victims. I grew up poor, so money has never been important to me. I learned the hard way what it was like to go without."

David looked over at The Traveler and asked, "And why did you set me free?"

"You and I are very much alike; solitary creatures. I have never told another living soul about my secret life. I never met anyone else who I could share my exploits with. I have been doing this for quite some time and before you, I never met another hunter.”

The Traveler could tell that David was intrigued. He had not been lying when he said he had never talked about his secret desires before, except of course with his victims and that was only done to terrify them.

“So did you free me so that you had someone to swap stories with?”

Shaking his head The Traveler replied, “No, I believed it was a true shame that someone with your talents would be put away for good. There is so much that we can teach each other.”

David let out a laugh. “You honestly think that you can teach me something?”

“Well, I haven’t been caught.”

“And just how have you managed that, *mon ami*?”

“Well, as you know, bleach destroys DNA, and I have disposed of several bodies in water. The water helps wash away any remaining trace evidence and if the bodies are found, it is difficult to pinpoint the actual disposal site. But mostly it is because I never stay in one place long. By the time the body is discovered, I am long gone.”

“And do you have proof of these so called ‘victims’?”

"Living in an RV it is hard to keep trophies, lack of space and all. Besides, very few prostitutes carry IDs but I have kept an occasional license and such."

"What about videotapes?"

Shaking his head, The Traveler answered, "No, I never invested in the equipment to do that."

"Ah, but when you record your ministrations it helps you to relive the event whenever you wish. Memories have a tendency to fade away."

David looked back to the closed door saying, "Speaking of memories fading away. It has been a while since I felt the warmth of blood on my hands, would it be possible to pay a little visit to your guest?"

The Traveler gave him a large grin. "By all means, please enjoy yourself. We can always share the next victim." As David headed back, The Traveler asked, "Would you please leave the door open so that I can listen to his screams as I drive though?"

"*Mais oui, mon ami*. That I can do."

The sounds coming from the prison guard as David released his pent up desires was pure music to The Traveler's ears. Yes, this may just turn out to be a perfect friendship.

***

Over the next few days, they slowly formed a brotherly bond, The Traveler decided to reveal his trophies to David. This helped prove to David that The Traveler did indeed share the same passion as him, just not quite at the same level yet.

One night, The Traveler divulged some of the harassment he endured growing up. As they made their plans for retribution, they agreed that it would be better if The Traveler drove during the day and David at night. Although David was indeed grateful to be free, he had yet to show a complete trust in The Traveler.

While The Traveler talked about his childhood, all David talked about was the various ways he wanted to kill. But then again, that was understandable - he'd had a year to do nothing but dream of things he could be doing.

As David thought about the havoc they were about to release on the unsuspecting victims, he patted The Traveler's shoulder, "*Mon ami*, call me by my trade name, The Hunter. After all, we are partners in crime now."

Chapter 3

The stifling heat and one hundred percent humidity confirmed that this was a typical summer day in Louisiana. Sheriff Jordan Hamilton was ecstatic that the transfer was complete and that David Thorguson would be Springport Prison's problem. However, without this case Alex Hamilton would not be part of her life. Two years ago, Jordan had been a detective with the Hope Police Department and she never suspected that her life would turn out like this. She always dreamed of being sheriff, but never considered that it would come to fruition.

While writing his book on David Thorguson, Alex had discovered a hidden passion in himself. The publisher anticipated the book would hit the bestseller list in record time. He ascertained the tranquility of Hope brought him the inspiration to write. Jordan was thankful that he decided to write, instead of rushing back to the FBI. He still consulted on cases but he could be here with her.

She looked up from the paperwork and noticed Detective Johnson approaching. "Sheriff, Springport Prison just called. They want to know when they can expect the prisoner."

Worried, she replied, "They should have been there hours ago. Where could they be?"

"I informed the Warden what time the van left. Should we dispatch a patrol car to see if the van had problems?"

"If there had been a problem, the guard would have radioed in. This is something else. Send Deputies Andrews and Williams, and you and I will also take a ride. The last thing we need is an escaped prisoner on our hands, especially David Thorguson. There is no way we want him back out terrorizing more women."

Before leaving the office, Jordan called the Warden personally. "Warden Russo, it's Sheriff Hamilton over in Hope. How well do you know this guard? Is he trustworthy?"

"Sheriff. Deputy Olivier is what we call a short timer; only working here until he is accepted into the state trooper's academy. He has previous military experience, Army I believe. He's been with us less than a year, but there have been no problems with his work. I don't see him running off with the prisoner, if that's what you are asking. For some reason, the GPS isn't working on the van and he isn't answering the radio or his cell phone. I just sent out two guards to look for him."

"I dispatched officers as well. Detective Johnson and I are also going to take a ride. It never hurts to have extra eyes out there looking. This is one prisoner we don't want to escape."

"Damn it! I never counted on encountering problems with just one prisoner."

"You should always expect the unexpected with Thorguson," Jordan replied.

***

It didn't take long for a multi-jurisdictional task force to be organized. Jordan quickly addressed everyone, "The individual we are looking for is cool and calculating; he planned this escape out carefully. David Thorguson and his accomplice have at least a four hour head start on us. From the tire tracks found near the abandoned transport van, preliminary reports indicate that the accomplice may be driving a motor home. As it stands, roadblocks have been initiated, and all vehicles are being searched, but more attention is being paid to motor homes. These two may have already left the state. If that is the case, it will complicate the search. I am calling in the FBI for assistance as soon as this meeting is over. However, I want these two caught before the feds arrive."

Chapter 4

Special Agent Jackson O'Riordan had been with the FBI for twenty years and assigned to the Behavioral Analysis Unit, BAU, for the last eighteen. He had seen plenty of homicides around the United States and, with experience, he learned to ascertain just from the crime scenes if they were dealing with a serial killer or not.

Recently, several cases involving the sexual orifices being super glued had caught his attention.   He had begun to suspect that a serial killer had been eluding detection for quite some time. This elusive killer traveled across the United States and killed mainly high risk men and women. He also found it highly unusual that none of the victims showed signs of sexual assault.

O'Riordan had collected photos, crime scene descriptions, lab and autopsy reports, and any other information on cases possibly committed by this mystery killer. While the torture performed on the bodies had variations, the use of super glue remained constant.

This particular killer never struck twice in the same place and showed obsessive compulsive tendencies. He could go months, even years, before the need to kill struck again. They had no clue as to the identity of this killer. His fingerprints had not been registered in any of the systems, meaning he had never been in the military or prison.

But for now, he had to put aside this case. Capturing David Thorguson was his top priority. He had carefully selected his task force. To help this task force understand what they were up against, when the team arrived in Hope, Louisiana they would watch a recorded interview between Alex Hamilton and David Thorguson. He also requested that Sheriff Hamilton make one of David Thorguson's homemade DVD's available. He wanted to reinforce the seriousness of the situation.

He would meet with Alex Hamilton when he arrived in Hope. With two killers on the loose, they had no time to waste. Before leaving for Hope, he made copies of any relevant information for Alex to peruse.

On the flight, while his task force reviewed their copies of the files, O'Riordan made notes of the more pertinent things he needed to discuss with everyone.

Chapter 5

Detective Michael Reese had been with the Mississippi State Police for twenty-three years. He had worked homicide most of those years, and could say retirement looked better with each passing year. When his cell phone rang at 3:30 a.m., he instantly knew it wasn't good.

"Reese."

"Detective, patrol found the body of a man at the Louisiana Mississippi state line. The body is in pretty bad shape, sir."

He let out a ragged breath. Being this close to the state line, he knew the FBI would more than likely become involved. "I'm heading out now."

After a quick shower, he donned a pair of jeans, shirt, and boots. Nothing fashionable, but comfortable. As he exited the bedroom, the smell of coffee reached him. When he entered the kitchen, he gave his wife a kiss and said, "I'm sorry. I didn't mean to wake you."

"Nonsense. I knew you would need a cup of coffee to wake up. I even fixed your favorite breakfast - egg and bacon on a bagel."

"What would I do without you?"

"Go broke from picking up fast food and coffee."

He laughed at that remark. "That's probably true. I don't know when I'll be back home."

"Don't worry about me. I'm going back to bed. Be careful."

Kissing her one more time, he headed out to see what the early morning hours brought.

***

By the time he arrived at the scene, red and blue flashing lights lit up the dark sky. Reese saw the news vans pulling in behind him and groaned. How had they managed to catch wind of this already? He didn't give it a second thought as he got closer to the crime scene.

A young officer managed the sign in sheet, while forensic techs worked the scene. "Officer, how is it going so far?" Reese asked, almost afraid of the response.

"All right, sir. It's bad, though. Officer Caulfield discovered the body of a naked man at the rest stop that wasn't there half an hour ago. One look at the body, and you could tell the man had been tortured."

Reese walked over to observe the body and grimaced. The victim was bludgeoned so badly that they would have to wait for fingerprint results.

Being this close to the Louisiana state line, he suspected they had located the missing prison guard.

If so, this also meant that they had an escaped convict and his partner in crime somewhere in this state, perhaps still in the area.

***

Once back at the precinct Reese located the Warden's number to inform him that he may have located the missing prison guard, even though he did not have confirmation.

Next he called Sheriff Hamilton. "Sheriff, sorry to bother you so early in the morning, but a body was found at a rest stop near the Louisiana/Mississippi state border, just inside of Mississippi."

"Have you identified the body?"

"It's in bad shape. We have to wait for fingerprint confirmation. I have a gut feeling it's the handiwork of your man, though."

"I'm on my way. I'll let the FBI agent working the case know."

"FBI is already involved then?"

"Yes. When he escaped, they offered their assistance. And we desperately need their resources to capture David Thorguson. Again."

***

Jordan called Agent O'Riordan after hanging up with Reese. "I know you and your team are still getting situated at the hotel, but a body has been found at the Mississippi state line that might be the missing guard. From what I understand, the body is in bad shape and it will take fingerprint confirmation to ID the body."

"I'll start that way now. Do you need a ride?"

"I can drive myself. That way you are free to do what you need to do."

"I'll see you at the crime scene then."

***

Dean Albright had been an investigative reporter for well over twenty years. He knew he was on to something as soon as he saw both Sheriff Hamilton and Special Agent O'Riordan arrive. Dean suspected that O'Riordan didn't like him, but he wasn't here to make any friends. Hell, no cop liked it when reporters showed up at a crime scene.

Earlier, Dean had put out feelers all over the surrounding states, in case a mutilated body turned up. He knew David Thorguson wouldn't be able to control himself now that he had escaped.

Dean quickly called out, "Agent O'Riordan, a moment please? Do you think this is the missing prison guard? Is that why you and Sheriff Hamilton are here?"

***

O'Riordan's skin crawled when he saw Dean Albright. He'd never had a good relationship with the media and Albright was one of the worst. O'Riordan had never found anything ethical in Albright's conduct. "No comment."

O'Riordan caught up with Sheriff Hamilton, and asked, "How are you feeling this morning?"

"I'm fine. I'm hoping for a quick confirmation on the body, so I can let his wife know. I don't want her to find out about this on the morning news. Even though they aren't supposed to release any names, that won't stop them from speculating."

"I just ran into Albright. That man gives me the creeps."

The responding officer was standing outside the bathroom and still collecting himself from the discovery. O'Riordan headed his way, and asked, "I take it you found the body?"

"Yes sir. They didn't even try to hide it. It was right by the park bench. Looked as if the body simply rolled out of the vehicle and they took off."

O'Riordan watched as a plain clothed detective walked over to where he and Sheriff Hamilton stood. "Sheriff Hamilton? I almost didn't recognize you."

She laughed as she rubbed her protruding stomach. "I've put on a few pounds since those press conferences regarding Thorguson. Detective Reese, this is Special Agent O'Riordan with the BAU. He is heading up the task force in search of David Thorguson."

The two men shook hands. "Agent O'Riordan."

"Detective Reese, it's nice to meet you. I only wish it was under different circumstances."

"Same here."

They stood in somber silence as they waited for forensics to finish gathering evidence. A crime scene tech bagged the corpse's hands, in case there was any evidence under the fingernails.

The coroner stood back up and informed them, "The man has been dead less than twelve hours. Bruising is evident on the wrists and ankles. Stab wounds and burn marks were also noted. He was tortured unmercifully. Ligature marks were found on the neck, indicating possible strangulation. However, no petechial hemorrhage was noted. Until the autopsy, the exact cause of death is unknown. With so much brutality done to the body, any one of the horrors could have caused his actual death."

***

Alex Hamilton was surprised how fast this last year had gone by. What started out as a sabbatical for him to interview David Thorguson, had turned into a life altering experience. At first, he thought he would miss profiling, but talking with David opened his eyes. David was the epitome of true evil and Alex believed he had been born evil. Alex wanted to continue his study on serial killers and the possibility that they were wired differently than everyone else.

Morning light poured into the conference room window as Alex reviewed the files O'Riordan had handed him. A rush of adrenaline built as he perused the documents and photos. He was happy with his new life and didn't realize how much he'd missed profiling. But was he ready to return to this line of work? In the past, the FBI had requested he return, but he wasn't certain he wanted to do this on a daily basis again.

O'Riordan asked, "Has anyone kept in touch with David Thorguson? Did he have an obsessive fan who wrote to him on a consistent basis? Perhaps someone wanted to emulate him or even worshipped him?"

"I was his ONLY visitor. David received very little mail," Alex replied. "I think most people were afraid to talk to him because of who he was. And what he did."

Alex recalled their past conversations. Thorguson bragged about how he'd kept the cops guessing. He enjoyed making himself sound superior to those around him. "David is a narcissist to the extreme and would have bragged about having a fan."

This was déjà vu. The conference room once again looked like a war room and Alex noticed that O'Riordan had already undone his tie and rolled up his shirtsleeves. As he finished reviewing the files, O'Riordan's hand-picked task force walked into the room for the meeting.

O'Riordan stood at the head of the table and made introductions, "Good afternoon everyone. I am FBI Special Agent Jackson O'Riordan and this is the all hands briefing for the capture of escaped convict David Thorguson task force." Waving his hand towards Alex, "I am sure you all know Alex Hamilton. Mr. Hamilton worked for the FBI in the past as a top profiler, and has interviewed Thorguson personally." Next, O'Riordan looked at the agent seated to his right, "Agent Kyle Manning will you please stand." As Manning stood, O'Riordan introduced him, "Agent Manning will be second in command."

O'Riordan walked over to the television that had previously been brought into the room and played one of the interviews between Alex and Thorguson first. "I wanted all of you to witness first hand just what you are up against."

After they had watched the interview and DVD, O'Riordan addressed the task force. "As you can tell, this is one psychopath we don't want free. Thorguson is a highly organized killer. He considers himself to be of superior intellect and extremely cunning. Do not put anything past him."

Sheriff Hamilton stood up and addressed the team. "I won't sugar coat this and say we will capture these two quickly."

O'Riordan nodded his head in agreement, and stated, "This will be a tiring task; you will work harder than ever before. Their capture will likely take weeks. Maybe even months. Forget about sleep and seeing your families. Our main focus is to capture these two individuals. I don't care how they are brought in. Dead or alive."

Alex looked at each man and woman and stated, "Tempers will be short, and morale low. Keep reminding yourself that it might be someone you know who is tortured and killed next. One guard has already been murdered and we want to prevent the body count from rising. No other case is more important to you than this one."

Sheriff Hamilton reminded the team, "This case is all over the news. The press is putting an extreme amount of pressure on us, wanting comments from those involved in the search. Please refer them to community relations; your only comment will be 'No Comment'. Due to all the publicity, the tip line is getting inundated with calls. All leads generated from these calls must be looked into, no matter how ridiculous the caller may sound."

O'Riordan added, "The FBI will air a prime time special Friday night asking for the public's help. Thorguson's mug shots and any possible disguises he may wear will be featured during the show. Sheriff Hamilton will have several of her own people helping man the tip lines that night, along with some volunteers who assisted during the first search."

Sheriff Hamilton handed out files to each person, "You will be divided up in twelve hour shifts. You will eat, drink, and sleep this case, until these two are brought in. No exceptions."

O'Riordan stressed. "These two had at least a four hour head start. A national alert has been issued to every town, county, and state law enforcement agencies with no hits yet. Thorguson has no other friends or family to turn to, that we know of. He has no reason to stay in or near Hope. We must figure out where they may be headed, and fast. Agent Manning will be in charge of the task force in Mississippi. All meetings will be teleconferenced. This is a team effort. No one task force is more important than the other."

Alex watched as everyone listened intently, and understood the seriousness of every word O'Riordan had to say. Alex didn't envy O'Riordan's job. It wasn't long ago that he was the one lecturing groups of FBI agents and other law enforcement personnel on a killer's profile. So it was interesting to watch this from the other side.

***

O'Riordan gave instructions to Agent Manning, "Check VICAP for any and all cases involving the sexual orifices being glued shut. Double check to see if I missed anything in the past. Once you compile your list we will compare notes." He continued, "We have learned from the coroner that the body found was the guard. The unsubs tortured and killed the guard before using super glue on his penis. I've been looking at a possible serial killer using this as a signature. If this is in fact the killer's signature, it may help us to get into his mind, or at least where he has been. It doesn't appear that he strikes the same area twice, which could prove helpful to us."

Agent Manning's curiosity was piqued. "I'll run it right now."

Nodding his head, O'Riordan reinforced his suspicions, "If I'm correct, and this is a serial killer, then we will have to send out a request asking all law enforcement agencies about murders involving super glue used in sexual orifices."

"Don't worry, sir, I know what to look for."

As he walked out the door, O'Riordan stated, "It doesn't matter what the time is, please call me with the results."

"Yes sir."

***

Several hours after the meeting had disbursed, Manning rushed into the conference room with an armful of papers. "O'Riordan, I found several more hits to super glue being used."

"Thanks Manning. I'll look over them now. Before leaving for Mississippi, double check that your help is not needed here."

O'Riordan sat down and opened his file containing the cases matching his requests from VICAP to compare to Agent Manning's results. He was so immersed in the files, he lost track of time. But the information that had been uncovered was almost as bad as what Thorguson had been doing.

This monster had been killing for well over ten years, with his MO barely changing over the years. No sexual penetration had been noted. The main change in the killings was that he refined his technique. The attacks had become more violent over the years; he was more adventurous in his torture techniques. For now, O'Riordan will stay in Hope until the sadistic duo struck again. He knew from experience that until these two were caught his home would be various hotel rooms, the exact location unknown even to him.

Chapter 6

Candy looked at herself in the mirror and was pleased with what she saw. Her best feature was her eyes; she had been told they were alluring, bedroom eyes. She had invested in a boob job to help compete with the younger girls. She needed this job to feed her costly coke habit.

She reveled in the power she had when dancing. These men couldn't take their eyes off of her. Most that came in here didn't know what to do with a naked woman. Hell, most of these weirdos probably never even saw a naked woman. As disgusting as the men could be, they had money. Besides, she loved teasing them. She liked the way it felt when their eyes roamed over her body, lingering on her breasts.

***

The Traveler entered the strip club on a mission and saw his next victim right away. The lights were dimmed and the music was blaring. She wore sheer pasties and her G-string had less material than if made with dental floss. The Traveler gave the woman on stage his full attention. She started to dance right in front of him, putting on a show for him. He had to hold back a laugh – if only she had an inkling of why he really wanted her. His skin tingled in anticipation of what he wanted to do to that body of hers. And it didn't involve sex.

Besides, there was no telling how many diseases he could catch from her.

He dug out a twenty dollar bill and tucked it into her G-string to catch her attention. He caught a whiff of her perfume, a heavy musky scent. She had a pouty expression on her face, as she moved closer to him. He would enjoy making her frown permanent, to hear her screams as he struck her with his whip and forced the flesh to peel away from her body with each lash. He could almost hear her pleas and desperate cries, begging for him to stop. He could feel his hands wrapping around her throat, slowly squeezing the life out of her.

"Come on, sugar, let's move this party to a back room."

This would give him a perfect opportunity to slip the drug into her drink. "Why don't you order some champagne for us? All this dancing must have you parched."

As she led him to the back he asked, "What's your name, honey?"

She let out a husky smoker's laugh and replied, "Candy with a 'y'. I'm sweet enough to eat."

"You look too young to work here."

She rolled her eyes. "You're not a narc or anything, are you? I don't need any trouble. Besides, sugar, I'm not all that young," she said as she straddled him. Her finger traced his jaw line as she settled in for a lap dance.

****

Candy felt as if her head was about to explode. She hadn't drank that much last night, but she woke up disoriented, unable to clear the fog from her head. She didn't even remember leaving the club.

She tried to sit up, but something prevented her from moving. She slowly forced her eyes open and saw a small amount of light seeping in from under the door frame. Panic burned through the fog in her head. *Where was she?*

As she waited for her vision to adjust to the darkness, terror coursed through her like molten lava. She needed to remain calm. Complete horror gripped her when she realized she was restrained to a bed. *What the hell?* She had found herself in some pretty dire situations before, but nothing like this. An eerie silence surrounded her.

A shadow moved in the faint light coming from beneath the doorway. Someone was out there. "Please help me. Is someone out there?" Her apprehension grew as her skin tingled from fear. "Please, I know someone is out there."

As the door opened, the man from the bar walked in. Surprise shot through her body. There had to be some mistake. The last thing she remembered was giving the guy a lap dance. He must have drugged her drink. What kind of game was he playing?

***

His eyes roamed over the woman on the bed. The torture he would unleash on her body turned him on more than her perfect little body. She couldn't be more than twenty-five years old. She may be young, but looking at her up close, she looked as if she had been ridden hard and put away wet. She wouldn't have to worry about growing old any longer. He doubted anyone would even miss her. Who would miss a harlot who sold her body for money?

A voice in his head told him to kill her now, but he ignored that voice. He wanted to have fun first.

The Traveler positioned a stool in front of her and pulled his sharpening stone and knife from his belt. With slow deliberation, he moved the blade along the stone, making sure she saw the glint of metal. He watched as her eyes were wide with fear as she followed each pass the blade made along the stone. Once finished, he ran it along the skin of his arm and shaved off a fine layer of hair. A smile of satisfaction formed across his face. "Perfect, don't you think? It should be sharp enough now."

"For what? " Her eyes glistened with fresh tears.

He rose to his feet to move the stool. "For us to have some fun."

***

Candy's mind raced with images of vicious, vile things he could do to her. Fear reignited her attempt to escape. A dozen promises and resolutions ran off her lips as she bartered with God to save her miserable life. She vowed to change her ways, to go on the straight and narrow if she lived. Then a miracle took place, she heard a commotion. Someone else was in the room. Had her prayers been answered? Was she saved?

The other person stood in front of her with a sneer on his face and her stomach coiled in surprise. He was also wielding a knife. He hadn't come to save her, but to join the creep in torturing her. She screamed in horror as he peered at her through dark, soulless eyes. Her heart beat so hard against her ribcage she swore the bones would break.

"Oh, sorry I didn't introduce you earlier. Candy with a 'y', this is my friend, The Hunter. He's going to keep you company as well."

She tried to look at the other man, but white hot pain tore through her body. Suddenly, a wire tightened around her neck. She struggled to gasp for air as her lungs began to feel like they were on fire.

She felt the strength leaving her body as blackness enveloped her. When she was about to pass out, the wire loosened a fraction. Only enough for her to gasp for some much needed air, and then the wire tightened again.

The monsters refused to stop. While one man raped her in ways she could never have imagined and tortured her with whips and knives, the other continued to tighten the wire around her neck. She was now lying on her stomach with her arms and legs restrained tightly behind her. Her muscles screamed in protest.

Her attackers were unrelenting. Why was this happening to her? Why didn't they allow her to die? She had lost track of time. Neither man let up. Instead, they continued to revive her.

She never realized the human body held so much blood. Surely, with losing the amount that she had, she should be dead. It seemed to coat the room, and it was all hers. There was no escape; no one would come to her rescue. She could feel the stickiness of the blood on her skin and smell its coppery scent. Stab wounds riddled her body, but none deep enough to kill her. Her tormentors were relentless, cutting her shallow enough to draw blood and cause her pain, but not fatal enough to allow death to free her from this place.

She whimpered when she saw them enter the room yet again. She attempted to hide her fear, but that had become an impossible feat. Fear had taken away all logical thinking. She couldn't stop thinking that this was all her fault, if only she had chosen a different path in life. Then, perhaps this wouldn't be happening to her.

*****

The Traveler had her hogtied in an unnatural position. After The Hunter had his fun with her, they inserted the meat hooks into her body to suspend her in the air and continued the torture.

The Hunter was pleased with how well they worked together. At first, he was afraid he wouldn't be able to perform in front of an audience, but he quickly overcame his fear. As he pulled out some of the woman's teeth, he informed The Traveler, "This is a little memento for me." However, The Hunter intended to send it to Sheriff Hamilton to let her know he was back in business.

Chapter 7

Dave Weaver had driven semi-trucks most of his life. He preferred driving at this hour of the night, when the roads were quiet. Looking up ahead, he watched as a motor home slowed down and something rolled out. He was making good time and curiosity got the best of him. Over the years he had found some good items discarded on the side of the road, which his wife sold over the internet for a nice profit.

As he walked down the dark hill, he began to think of all the things this package could be. The heavy underbrush and vines tended to tangle around his feet. The package must weigh a pretty good bit to roll through this mess.

One look at his find and he nearly lost his supper. He rushed back to his truck, pulled out his revolver, locked his doors, and called 911.

***

Detective Ken Jameson spotted the lights of the eighteen wheeler up ahead. One of the officers came up to him as he stepped out of his vehicle. "Sir, it would be easier to get to the crime scene from the apartment complex. It is a pretty steep incline this way."

"Thanks. Get on the radio and have dispatch inform the forensic techs and coroner."

The apartment complex turned out to be a gated community. Management wouldn't be too happy about cops swarming all over the complex and worrying the tenants. But they would have to deal with it – murder was more important than upsetting the residents.

The guard shack matched the buildings surrounding it, blending into the landscape. When he pulled up, he flashed his badge.

The guard looked at the badge and said, "Detective, follow this road straight back. I've already had a few calls, so I'm sure there will be some Lookie Lu's watching."

"Thanks. We'll try not to cause your residents too much inconvenience."

It wasn't hard to miss the access point of the crime scene from the complex. A crowd had begun to form around the patrol cars.

Ken kept his head down as he approached the scene, ignoring the whispers and questions that were being tossed out at him. Almost as soon as he ducked under the yellow tape, an officer came up to him.

"Detective, the coroner called to say they are a few minutes out. The body has to be carried out; the terrain is too rough for the gurney. It's a damn nightmare. I've never seen a case like this before."

***

Doctor Meghan Cook had been with the State of Mississippi's Medical Examiner's Office for ten years and had worked this county for seven of those years. She had thrown on a pair of jeans and T-shirt, instead of her normal office attire, and for once wore sensible shoes. She pulled her hair into a high ponytail before stepping out of the vehicle.

Detective Jameson walked up to her as she stepped out of her car. "Doc, I almost didn't recognize you. I've never seen you dressed casual."

She laughed at his comment. "When the call came in, your officer informed me it was in a wooded area."

As they walked over to the body, she immediately pointed out some details. "Ligature marks are present on her wrists and ankles. Stab and burn wounds riddle her body. Several of the wounds have begun to crust over and some bruises are the shade of an eggplant, indicating they have started to heal. The killer tortured this woman for days, not hours. I'm not sure about these puncture wounds, some are through and through."

"How long has she been dead, Doc?"

"Rigor hasn't begun to set in. I'd say a couple of hours at most. I'll know more after the autopsy."

Dr. Cook tried to keep her emotions under control when working a case, but she still felt for this poor woman. This killer sadistically tortured her for days and once she died, he tossed her aside like a piece of trash.

Detective Jameson knelt down by the body to get a closer look. "Let's make sure we bag the hands, in case she fought back."

"Always," Dr. Cook informed Jameson, "There are no defensive wounds. I will put a rush on the toxicology results. There is petechial hemorrhaging in the eyes, bruising around the neck. The bruising indicates that he sexually assaulted her - vaginally and anally; plus it looks like he used some kind of glue afterwards. That may be an important detail. There are so many cuts though, that I won't know until I perform the autopsy if exsanguination or strangulation was the cause of death. Several of the wounds are shallow, but these on her abdomen appear to be deeper. He wanted to cause intense pain before killing her. As far as the breast mutilation, her blood was still pumping when he removed them. You can tell from the blood stains." Dr. Cook carefully opened the victim's mouth and said, "He also removed a couple of teeth."

"The killer displayed a lot of rage. We need to look at the boyfriend, husband, or some man in her life."

Dr. Cook kept her thoughts to herself, but the glue bothered her. She remembered a recent case where a prison guard had been found with his genitalia super glued.

***

Once back to her office, she did a quick search to find out who was in charge of that case, Special Agent Jackson O'Riordan. Against her better judgment, she called to talk to him about this case.

"Agent O'Riordan, my name is Dr. Meghan Cook. I am a coroner here in Mississippi. I may be overstepping my bounds, but I am working a case here that resembles your VICAP request. The young lady had super glue used on her, vaginally and anally. However, there are also signs of sexual assault and severe mutilation. The killer also removed both breasts."

"Dr. Cook where did you say you are located?"

"I'm in Hampton, Mississippi."

"I have a temporary office here in Hope, Louisiana."

"You aren't that far from me, maybe three hours at the most."

"Dr. Cook, would it be possible for us to meet in person?"

"Yes, we can. I will be performing the autopsy on the victim shortly."

"Wait a minute, do you mean to tell me that this is a new case?"

"Yes, sir, it is. I just picked up the body this morning."

"Doctor, can you please give me your exact address? I'm on my way there now."

***

Dr. Cook's appearance surprised O'Riordan. She didn't resemble the other coroner's he had met. She was much younger than he expected. She stood five-two in heels; he always pictured doctors as being taller for some reason. She had a determination in her eyes, and he suspected she would be a firecracker to handle. Her blue eyes contrasted well with her dark hair. "Dr. Cook? I'm Agent O'Riordan and this is Alex Hamilton. He is the profiler who worked on the David Thorguson case."

"Pleased to meet you both. We seldom get this savage of a murder here, much less two in a matter of days. The prison guard's murder was a few towns over, but it still happened in this state. The glue is too much of a coincidence not to be considered. I don't believe that a jealous boyfriend or husband killed this woman. A vicious person, someone who has done this before, committed this atrocity. The cuts are too precise."

"I will keep your name out of it for now. I don't want to piss anyone off right from the start. Let's see what you have, and go from there."

Dr. Cook looked at O'Riordan thoughtfully. "I certainly appreciate that. I know Detective Jameson. You will have to take this slowly; he won't welcome you with open arms. He already has his suspicions on who committed this murder and isn't open to insights on his cases. That man can be quite stubborn at times."

O'Riordan knew he would run into some obstacles along the way, so this wasn't a surprise. "I take it he doesn't like when you offer advice."

"No, he wants my reports straight and to the point. He doesn't take kindly to me butting into his cases, so I'm not sure how he will handle a federal agent inquiring about one. However, I don't want any more bodies ending up in my morgue if I can help it."

O'Riordan spoke slowly, picking each word carefully, "Dr. Cook, I'm working on a theory here that maybe you can help me with. I suspect that a serial killer has been flying under the radar for quite some time."

"Let me guess, the signature was the super glue?"

"That's my part of my theory. Most bodies have been dumped right off the interstate, in rest areas or campgrounds."

"Now you have the signatures of two separate killers on one body."

"I hope that I'm not spinning my wheels on this theory, but I'm worried since these two have combined forces, they will be a force to be reckoned with." O'Riordan had begun to sound like a broken record, but this case was getting the better of him today.

He had a bad hunch that these murders were connected. In the past, his gut had never failed him. He could tell Dr. Cook was thinking about all the information he'd dumped on her.

"Did you bring any files with you by chance?" Dr. Cook asked, sounding intrigued.

"I did. I take it you would like to see what I have collected so far."

"Let's go to my office. We will have more room there."

"If my theory is correct, then this killer only strikes once in each place. He kills and moves on to another town, which may be one of the reasons he goes undetected."

Her office was exceptionally tidy, which surprised O'Riordan. He had expected to find an overflowing inbox. She noticed him looking over her office and explained, "I'm a bit of a neat freak and tend to keep my desk clutter free. I even labeled the inboxes and outboxes so that my secretary can find what she needs. I don't work well in chaos. Can I get you a coffee or an espresso, before we sit down?"

She had an espresso machine, as well as a single cup coffee maker with an assortment of coffees and teas, a microwave, and a small refrigerator. "You must pull some long hours here," Alex remarked.

"I do. I try to make it home around seven, but that isn't always the case. I decided to make the office a little more convenient for me several years back. The one thing I missed was the lack of a coffee shop here in town. I ordered an espresso machine the day after I moved here. I can live without all the restaurants, but I am addicted to my espressos. The first morning I set it up I think I made twenty lattes for staff members. I've created coffee monsters here. Someone is always bringing in new coffee syrups to try.

"I've also learned what several of the detectives like to drink and try to keep that on hand. I find when breaking bad news to a loved one, it helps if you have something available to keep their hands occupied. Something about rolling a cup in your hands, tends to offer a slight distraction from the heartbreaking news."

Alex took her up on the espresso, where O'Riordan settled for a soda, and then they gathered around the table in Meghan's office. O'Riordan arranged several photos and autopsy reports for her perusal. He had reviewed the case so often; he had every word committed to memory. She looked at each photo with objectivity, looking beyond the mutilation for clues that the murders could be committed by the same person.

The dread that had been building in him settled heavy in his mind as Dr. Cook and Alex reviewed the files. He feared David Thorguson and his new found partner were already on the hunt again, but where? Were they still in Mississippi or had they moved on to another state? When Dr. Cook looked up from the files she said, "I agree with you. There are too many similarities in these murders for them not to have been committed by the same person."

O'Riordan wanted Dr. Cook on the task force. She had an instinct about her that they would need. "Dr. Cook, I would like for you to join the task force. I don't expect you to traipse all over the country with us, but we could use your input."

"I have no problem with it. I have some vacation time that I can use, so this shouldn't be an issue."

"Well then, welcome aboard. Let's get this guy."

***

The following morning O'Riordan called Detective Jameson. "Detective Jameson, my name is Special Agent Jackson O'Riordan with the FBI. I received a hit earlier this morning on one of my notices, stating that you had a murder that matches a serial killer I am on the lookout for."

O'Riordan could sense Detective Jameson's guard immediately going up. "Look Agent O'Riordan, I don't know how you found out about the case, but it is still under investigation. As of now, we haven't identified the victim. With the amount of rage this killer showed, I am leaning towards an ex-boyfriend or husband. I have your number if I believe you should be updated on the case."

"Detective, please hear me out. If I am correct, this killer won't strike your town again, he has already moved on. These killers have no remorse and torture their victims relentlessly before killing them."

"Agent O'Riordan, I wish I had something to give you, but right now there isn't much. You are more than welcome to review what evidence we have so far."

"Thank you, Detective. I'll be at your office shortly. Detective, even if you don't want my help, please at least let the FBI labs help analyze the evidence. I will have them put a rush on everything for you."

***

Crap, the man was already in town. There went his day.

Detective Jameson didn't want, or need, the FBI's help in solving the murder, but he would accept O'Riordan's offer to use the FBI's lab.

He had all the information regarding the murder laid out on the conference room table for O'Riordan. Jameson watched as he studied the pictures. "This is one twisted SOB. We identified the victim this morning after getting off the phone with you. The name she gave the police officer who arrested her for prostitution was 'Candy'. I plan on going to the strip club to see if perhaps she pissed off a customer. Maybe she screwed the wrong john, pissed off a pimp, or had a boyfriend on the side who despised what she did. The possibilities are endless on a suspect pool."

***

O'Riordan kept quiet. After reviewing the information, the mutilation could have been committed by both men. They each killed high risk victims, thinking no one would miss them. Only some of these women did have families, loved ones that missed them. At least they had a partial name to go with the body.

O'Riordan had his work cut out for him. As Dr. Cook had suggested, Jameson was very territorial. He seemed to be extremely resentful of the FBI's interference. Why didn't the man see reason? Jameson had his mind set on the fact that a jealous lover killed her.

He knew all about stroking egos, but damn, he didn't have time for that. Right now, it would be best to take the position that he came to observe and lend a helping hand. Except the killers may already be on the prowl, and they had no idea where they were.

He kept trying to get into the mind of the killer, or now killers, but he was getting nowhere. If he could figure out where the killer abducted his previous victims, he might get a better insight into his hunting ground.

Chapter 8

The Skylark Inn left a lot to be desired. The current remodel did little to help the old motel, the rooms still felt cramped. The carpet and furnishings were old, but at least it was clean and the bed was new and comfortable. O'Riordan had slept in worse places over the years. Even though Alex had offered to stay in town with him, O'Riordan could tell that he wanted to get back home to his wife. So he was on his own for the night, unless something else happened.

He set up his laptop on the small table in the room. There was no desk or good workspace, but they offered Wi-Fi. He needed to work on a timeline, showing where the killer had been. This may help them figure out where they were headed next.

O'Riordan noticed the take out menus by the phone and decided that after his shower, he would see what they had to offer and settle in for the night. As he discarded his jacket on a chair, he heard a knock at his door. He looked through the peephole and was surprised to see Dr. Meghan Cook standing in the hall.

"I thought you may like some company. I heard through the grapevine that Jameson wasn't very cooperative."

He shouldn't let her in. But when he looked into her eyes, he forgot about the intense loneliness he felt; the all-consuming stress of his job, and the chaos of his life. Instead, he felt a sudden desire to pull her into his arms and make love to her all night. It could cause a problem if they became involved. He had never been good at relationships, and when you throw in the long distance, it was doomed for failure.

"I was about to jump in the shower and then order takeout. Did you need me for something?" He didn't mean to sound rude, but her presence had him on guard for some reason.

"I can do better than takeout. Let's go to my house and I'll fix us some supper. Afterwards, we can go over the case."

"You don't have to do that."

"I know, but I want to. I'm a rather good cook, if I do say so myself. Besides, I already have lasagna in the oven. Who can say no to lasagna?"

"I hate to see good food go to waste, and Italian food is a favorite of mine."

O'Riordan thought he had the good doctor pegged, until he saw what she drove. A 1994 Porsche 911 Cabriolet convertible. He became aroused just thinking of her handling all the power that car had under its hood. Meghan must have seen the envy in his eyes and laughed. "I like the speed and to feel the wind in my hair. Thankfully, I know most of the state troopers around here. Would you like to drive it?"

Despite the tempting offer to drive her car, he followed Meghan to her house. On the way over, he noticed the sunset and its fiery orange hues. He couldn't remember the last time he sat outside to enjoy the sunset. It enraged him at the very thought that somewhere out there, David Thorguson and his accomplice could be looking at the same sunset as him. It was a gorgeous night and all he could think about was this damn case.

The timer was going off as they walked through the door. The tantalizing aroma teased their senses. He didn't realize how hungry he was until his mouth started watering. "It smells wonderful. I'm starving."

Laughing, she replied, "Well then, let's eat while everything is hot."

As Meghan led the way into the kitchen, they talked about the weather and kept the conversation away from the case. She served them each a big helping of lasagna while O'Riordan poured them a nice glass of Chianti. Meghan placed a basket of breadsticks and a bowl of salad in the middle of the table for them to share. "Help yourself."

He watched in fascination as she dug into her supper, savoring every bite. "Food is my escape. I see so much death that I tend to turn to food. Cooking has turned into a pastime for me. I enjoy finding a new recipe to try. I like the challenge of preparing the more difficult recipes, while I am working on a mind boggling case. It helps me concentrate on something else and then a solution creeps into my mind before I have realized it.”

“That’s good advice. I may have to try it since this case has me stumped.”

“This is a really psychotic duo running loose. Death is too good for them.”

“David Thorguson is a psychopath. Neither man left many clues before, but now it’s as if they don’t care. Neither man is a dummy though. Until Thorguson’s accomplice helped him escape, he was a ghost. It was by chance that I even realized a possible serial killer traveled from state to state, never killing in the same place. I just wish I knew where they were going next. If the accomplice keeps to his pattern of not killing in the same city, then we know where they aren’t going. That still leaves a vast amount of ground to cover. With them traveling across the country in a motor home, they don’t have to stop and find a hotel room. That makes it even more difficult to track their movement.”

She thought about what he had said. “Your best bet may be to warn not only the police, but as many of the coroners’ offices as you can as well.” Looking him in the eyes, she explained, “Trust me, we are a close knit bunch who talk.”

"I will keep that in mind." Taking another bite of lasagna he said, "Now, let's enjoy this wonderful supper you made."

***

After supper, they moved into the living room. "How long have you been with the FBI?" she asked while sitting next to him on the couch, making it difficult for him to concentrate. He watched as she tucked her feet underneath her and turned toward him. He could feel the warmth of her skin, her knee barely touching his.

Clearing his throat, he answered, "Too long, too many cases."

She looked damned sexy sitting there. O'Riordan found himself wondering what it would be like to reach over and kiss her.

"We shouldn't be doing this." O'Riordan kept telling himself this was a bad idea, but he had a hard time seeing the reasoning behind it.

"Why Special Agent O'Riordan? We are two single adults, am I correct?"

"Yes, but it could get messy."

"Only if we let it." She kissed him, pulling him towards her as she did.

It felt so good to touch her, to kiss her. It was better than he ever imagined in his wildest dreams. His arms wrapped around her, picking her up.

"I'm too old for this teenager stuff. Where's the bedroom?"

"Down the hall, first door on the right."

By the time they made it to the bedroom, a trail of clothes were scattered behind them. He gazed down at her tanned body. In one swift movement, they were on the bed and he was on top of her, kissing and fondling. She let out a sensual moan and arched up to meet him.

She lightly raked her hand along his chest and abdomen. She could feel where his body was riddled with scars as a result of his career.

She slowly kissed each one, as if trying to kiss away the pain.

***

The tantalizing scent of cooking bacon and coffee woke Meghan. Desire built up inside her once again as the memory of O'Riordan moving inside her was still intense. She couldn't believe he was preparing breakfast for her. She quickly dressed and headed towards the kitchen.

"I'm impressed, an agent that can cook."

Giving her a deep good morning kiss, he smiled and answered, "There are a lot of things I'm good at in the morning, but I thought you may want to eat something first."

After pouring them a cup of coffee, she made herself comfortable at the bar and watched him finish. As he handed her a plate of scrambled eggs and bacon, her mouth was already watering – but it wasn't for food.

***

Detective Jameson had taken O'Riordan up on his offer to use the FBI labs. When the toxicology report came back, it confirmed that the victim did have Rohypnol in her system. O'Riordan was leaning towards bars being one of the main playgrounds for this serial duo. With so many people around, it would be easy to slip something in a drink without being noticed. And no one would think twice about a man assisting a drunk person out of the bar.

Their perp had to be a real smooth talker to be able to abduct men and women. Men tended to be more standoffish when it came to another man approaching them. To attract women easily, he was probably good looking.

O'Riordan wondered why the body wasn't posed; David Thorguson's ego fed on attention. He loved playing his cat and mouse game, posing the bodies, knowing that there was no trace evidence left behind.

Self-preservation must be more important than
taunting the police right now.

Chapter 9

Sheriff Hamilton looked at the package that arrived in today's mail. The small box had no return address and was postmarked Brisby, Mississippi.

She decided to call Alex, "Alex, I received a package in the mail with no return address. It was mailed from Mississippi."

"Have you opened it yet?" Alex asked.

"No. I'm afraid to find out what's inside. It rattles when shaken, so I don't think it's a body part. It's too small to be a bomb."

"I'm on my way over. Don't open it until I get there."

***

Alex found Jordan at her desk, staring at the small package. He walked around the desk and carefully picked it up.

When he opened it, he found a note folded up inside the box along with two teeth. "I'm afraid to see what it says."

Alex read the note quickly.

"A memento from my first adventure. Love, The Hunter."

Rage coursed through him. He didn't like that Jordan was being brought back into this case by David, especially with her being pregnant. However, he liked his manhood and had no desire to say anything to her. When her Cajun temper lit, look out. Alex picked up the phone to call O'Riordan to inform him about the newest development.

"O'Riordan, this is Alex. Jordan received an unmarked package from David Thorguson. It contained a couple of teeth and a note. The postmark was from Brisby, Mississippi."

Chapter 10

Stan and Tori Donovan were finally going on vacation. It had taken them years to save up and they were extremely excited about it. Neither had been to Williamsburg, Virginia and they couldn't wait to absorb the history there. From Williamsburg, they planned on traveling to Washington, D.C. to visit the Smithsonian.

They pulled over at a rest stop on the outskirts of a small town in North Carolina to stretch their legs. It was pitch black outside and very few lights were on.

"I sure hope the restrooms are unlocked."

"You and me both," replied Tori, "I don't have the luck of going behind a building and whipping it out."

"Maybe we should call it a night and find a hotel?"

"I can drive for a while. I've been napping for the past few hours. I'm good to go after I pee," Tori said.

"Babe, grab the flashlight out of the glove box. Looks like this rest stop might be under construction."

Tori had an uneasy feeling about this place. "Stan, I think I can wait. Let's wait and see if we find a fast food restaurant or something else up ahead. This place is creepy."

"Don't be silly. There is no one else around."

Tori swore eyes were watching them. She glanced behind her as they walked towards the restrooms. She didn't see anything but the emptiness of the night. "Come on Stan, let's get out of here."

"I'm right here. I'll even go in with you. Trust me, there's no one else around." She gripped Stan's hand tighter as they headed towards the restrooms. She swore something moved in the shadows.

"Christ, Tori, ease up. There's nothing to worry about."

"I can't help it. I swear someone is out there." She strained to peer deeper into the night. Nothing was visible. Maybe she was being paranoid.

On their way back, they noticed a motor home parked right beside them. Stan said in an irritated voice, "Why the hell did he park there? It's not like there aren't a million other spots he could have parked the blasted thing."

***

Tori wasn't sure where she was. A man was in front of her. She tried to focus in on his face and her surroundings when she noticed something gleaming in his hand. She focused on his face again and shivered at the sight of his dark and soulless eyes. She could feel the evil emitting from him.

Tori knew they were going to die. The sudden realization filled every molecule of her body. "I'm glad you are awake. My friend and I are going to take turns with you and your husband. He can have his fun with your husband while I have my chance at you."

Terror tore through her body. She heard a deep moaning. "Stan, is that you?"

Her captor moved closer. "Now, where should I start? I've found a delightful new trick that I've added to my techniques. I want to carve you inside and out, similar to a turkey on Thanksgiving Day. The human body really fascinates me. The first ones that I played with, I never thought about the inside of their body. "

"Me, I like to start cutting into your pretty little flesh, slowly at first. Causing you just enough pain to make you uncomfortable. After a while, I'll increase the pain. On the other hand, my partner hasn't learned complete self-control. He is still practicing. Listen. You can tell from your husband's screams."

Tori noticed that Stan's moans had indeed turned into blood curdling screams. Tears rolled down her face, as the knife slipped into her flesh. The red hot pain was like nothing she had ever experienced. Tori felt the blackness taking over as she lost consciousness.

***

Officer Gavin Daniels found it difficult to fight the drowsiness that always seemed to plague him these last few hours of night watch. Daybreak would be here soon, but not soon enough. By 6:00 a.m., he would be back at the station, but first he and his partner, Officer Russ Bass, had to complete checking the rest stops in this area. This had to be the most boring part of the job, checking each rest stop every half hour on the dot. The Governor put the initiative through, after constituents expressed a concern that they didn't feel safe stopping at them at night. Instead of hiring a nighttime security guard, it was determined that an extra shift would suffice for the state troopers. Everyone took turns with the shifts, although, Daniels preferred running radar at night.

Bass was already dozing off. "Almost done. It has been an extremely uneventful night."

Bass nodded his head in agreement. "I don't think I've seen anyone out tonight."

"It has to be because of this weather." The rain had stopped, but it left the air muggy. A thick haze blanketed the still gray sky.

"I'm ready to call it a day. At least our shift is almost up. I'm ready for a vacation, find a deserted beach and drink my worries away."

"You sound like my wife. She is bugging me to go to the beach. As if I want to deal with people. If I go somewhere, I want to go to a mountain getaway. Maybe hike or fish, as long as no people are around."

"Hell, you think you got it bad, my wife is bugging the crap out of me to take her and the kids to Orlando. They want to see the attractions there. Can you imagine what the crowds will be like?"

As they turned into the rest stop, they noticed a Jeep Cherokee parked in the lot.

Daniels pulled up next to the Jeep and asked, "I don't see anyone around, do you?"

"Nope. Maybe they are in the restroom."

Daniels had a gut feeling that their night was about to turn sour. "I have a bad feeling about this one. Let's go take a look."

"Sure, why not? It's not like we have anything else to do."

The men's restroom was empty. Knocking on the women's restroom door, they announced themselves. "State Troopers coming in to do a routine check. Is anyone in here?"

No response.

Now Daniels knew his gut feeling was right. He radioed in for dispatch to run the plates. He found out that the Jeep belonged to a Stan and Tori Donovan. He called it in to inform that an abandoned car had been found. A small search team was organized to search the surrounding area. Search and Rescue even brought out some dogs, but they were not found. It was like they disappeared into thin air.

Chapter 11

Jason and Evan Albright's parents thought it would be a perfect family vacation if they went camping. Their parents could be so lame. Nobody went camping anymore, they stayed in hotels instead.

Jason begrudgingly admitted the place was kind of cool though. But he would never admit that to his parents. There were all kinds of trails and woods to explore. Their dad even bought a metal detector to look for buried treasures. Jason would be thirteen this year, where Evan was only ten, still a baby. Besides, Evan was a momma's boy.

"Come on, Evan, let's go. Mom and Dad said we could hike a little further up, as long as we bring the walkie talkie with us. There has to be some neat stuff buried in the woods."

Jason didn't wait for Evan as he took off running. He heard Evan call out, "Wait up. I'm coming. Come on, Jason, stop!"

"Hurry up," Jason hollered as he galloped through the undergrowth, already venturing off of the trail.

Jason rolled his eyes when he heard Evan whine like a big baby. "Come on, Jason, wait up." Jason slowed down, so Evan didn't go back and tattle tell. When Evan finally caught up with Jason, they spotted a rabbit darting through the bushes. They made their way through the overgrown game trail, walking around tall pine trees and heavy brush. This was an adventure to them, and they giggled as they ran after the rabbit. It didn't take the rabbit long before he became tired of the boys' chasing game and darted down a hiding hole.

As they walked back the way they came, Jason turned on the metal detector. Finding nothing, he wondered if this had been a lame idea. No one probably ventured this far off the trails anyhow.

Evan walked ahead of him to throw sticks, even lamer. "Jason, come check this out. It looks like someone tried to burn something."

"Cool, I wanna see." Pushing Evan out of the way, he looked at what his brother had found, "Evan, I think someone tried to set up a camping spot back here. Maybe we will find something." The smell didn't bother the boys, but what they found was far more than they ever bargained for. Jason almost passed out and Evan began to throw up. From the look of the bodies, they had been there for a while. However, Jason didn't want to take a chance. He grabbed Evan and pulled him away from the bodies. "Come on, let's go."

Jason tried his dad on the walkie talkie, "Dad, you there? Dad, come in. We're in trouble, big trouble!"

His dad's panicked voice came over the walkie, "What is it? Boys, are y'all okay?"

"Evan found some dead bodies. They are gross, Dad. They don't even look human, their skin is all weird."

"Where are y'all?"

"We're in the woods, off the trail by the trailer. Please hurry, Dad."

***

The coroner arrived at the same time as the crime scene techs. After a quick inspection of the bodies, he walked over to Detective Rick Bankston. "I did a quick examination of the bodies. You may want to contact the FBI. This may be the work of the escaped convict they are looking for down in Louisiana. It has been all over the news, and this appears to be their killers' work. There's a lot of torture and mutilation."

"When will you be doing the autopsy?"

"My techs are about to load up the bodies and I plan to perform the autopsy once we are back at the morgue."

Nodding his head, Bankston replied, "I will meet you there as soon as I can, Doc."

***

Bankston headed to the coroner's office. He had left a message with the local FBI office about the most recent murder, and hoped to hear from an agent soon. The Potomac County Coroner's Office was attached to the morgue, located in the basement of the County Hospital.

The odor of death hit him as soon as he opened the doors to the autopsy room. Bankston dreaded this part of the job; the smell of formaldehyde got him every time.

Dr. Brad Welsh greeted him with a nod. The bodies were laid out on gurneys; water still glistened off of them from the recent wash down. With the bodies being freshly cleaned, the amount of torture that these two endured became more apparent.

Dr. Welsh explained, "The decomposition of the bodies is bad, but I did determine the cause of death for the man. Exsanguination, but I'm still working on the cause of death for the female. It is probably exsanguination for her as well. Several ribs were broken and I believe both were revived several times, before they finally succumbed to death. The woman was sexually assaulted, but not the man. Severe mutilation occurred to the genital area of the woman. I'm thinking he penetrated her with a foreign object, possibly a knife. The attacker didn't bother wearing a condom. Semen was found around the vagina, anus, and on her thighs. The samples have already been sent to the lab. Restraint marks are evident at the wrists and ankles on both bodies. The man had horrendous amounts of mutilation performed on his body. Each body has deep puncture wounds that nicked their lungs. It would have caused them to gurgle, struggling to breathe.

"Time of death was likely seventy-two hours ago. Rigor has left the bodies and decomposition has begun. I found two burn marks on each body, consistent with the use of a Taser. This is most probably how he subdued both victims."

"It looks as if this killer wanted the torture to last as long as possible," Bankston said.

Dr. Welsh agreed. "That's my conclusion. The fatal wounds came several days later, maybe when it became harder to revive them. It is evident from the wound pattern that the torture lasted for days. This killer wanted them to suffer a great deal before killing them. All major organs were avoided in the beginning. This killer has a basic knowledge of anatomy or has been practicing, learning how to torture his victims. The knife wounds are precise. He showed a great deal of control, performing the horrendous torture and not killing them for several days. As soon as I receive the toxicology results, I will provide you with my written report."

Bankston called the officer that found the abandoned car. "Officer Daniels, my name is Detective Bankston. I'm working the murders of the owners of the vehicle you found abandoned at a rest stop off I-64. It is a 2000 Jeep Cherokee."

"Yes sir. We have the vehicle stored in our impound lot, if you are interested. When I noticed the abandoned vehicle, my partner and I checked the restrooms and the immediate area to try and locate them. We came up empty handed. Search and Rescue were called out to check the woods surrounding the rest stop, but that search also yielded no results."

"Was the car dusted for prints?"

"No sir. It was just impounded. It has been sitting here ever since."

If Dr. Welsh was correct and the FBI was involved, this case would become multi-jurisdictional after all. "Would it be possible to have the car dusted?"

"I don't see why not."

***

Detective Bankston was working at his desk when Officer Daniels called back. "Detective Bankston, I have some surprising news for you. I'm guessing the perps either didn't worry about fingerprints or could care less, but we found two sets of fingerprints that did not match those of the victims. One set is unknown, but the other belongs to an escaped prisoner by the name of David Thorguson. I have already let the FBI know. An Agent O'Riordan will be contacting you, I am sure."

"Thank you, Officer. I'll be on the lookout for his call."

How did an escaped convict from Louisiana make it all the way up here, and was he still in the area? Bankston decided to do a little research on this fellow. The best place to start was to call the arresting officer, Detective Jordan Sanders.

"My name is Detective Bankston with Potomac County Sheriff's Department. May I speak to Detective Jordan Sanders about the David Thorguson case?"

"This is Sheriff Hamilton; you want to talk about David Thorguson?"

"Yes ma'am. I would like to talk to the lead detective."

"That would be me. Since the arrest, I've been elected sheriff of Hope and married. It's been a busy year. What can I help you with?"

"I was wondering if we could get a copy of your case file on David Thorguson. David's fingerprints have shown up on a related case here and I want to know what I am dealing with."

"Where did you say you are at again?"

"I'm with Potomac County Sheriff's Department in North Carolina."

"I can have a copy expressed to you this morning. If you provide me with your email address, I will send you the most pertinent information."

"I appreciate it."

"Detective, be careful. This SOB is slippery as hell."

***

O'Riordan called Dr. Cook, "Dr. Cook, how would you like to take a ride with me? They have a body that matches our profile in North Carolina."

"They aren't leaving much of a cooling off period between victims are they?"

Shaking his head, "No, David more than likely has a lot of pent up desires he wants to unleash."

She asked, "When did you want to leave?"

"I'll pick you up at your house. Pack a bag in case we stay longer than intended. And don't worry about missing work, the Director already called your supervisor and informed him that you would be assisting us with a high profile case."

***

After picking Dr. Cook up at her house, they took the FBI jet to North Carolina. O'Riordan was glad that the Director had given him permission to use it as he saw fit to get to the crime scenes. This would save them on the travel time, and they'd arrive at the scenes quickly.

When they landed, the local FBI office would have a vehicle waiting at the tarmac.

Three hours after receiving the phone call, O'Riordan and Cook were driving to the Potomac County Sheriff's Department. At the front desk O'Riordan introduced himself, "I am Special Agent Jackson O'Riordan and this is Dr. Meghan Cook. We are here to see Detective Bankston."

"Yes sir, please have a seat and I will let him know you are here."

***

It never even occurred to Detective Bankston that Agent O'Riordan would just show up, he figured he would just call and touch base.

He walked up to the front desk to greet O'Riordan. "Agent O'Riordan, it is a pleasure to meet you."

Shaking hands, O'Riordan introduced Dr. Cook, "This is Dr. Cook, she works for the State of Mississippi Coroner's office, but has agreed to help us with this case.

"Dr. Cook, it is nice to meet you as well." Looking at O'Riordan, he stated, "As I am sure you are aware, we do have confirmation that David Thorguson's prints were found at the scene. The other set has yet to be identified."

"May we set up a task force here?"

"I've already cleared everything with my captain. We want to help you all anyway we can."

Two more agents entered the conference room with several boxes. They began setting up maps and photos on one of the bulletin boards in the room. "The yellow tacks indicate murders that we suspect have been committed by the accomplice. The red indicates the murders we suspect have been committed by both the accomplice and Thorguson. If we determine where they have been, maybe we can track their next movements."

Bankston looked at the photographs going up and all of the highlighted places on the map. "All of these cases?"

"I'm still sorting through case notes, but yes, it appears Thorguson's accomplice has been operating for quite some time now. It worries me that these two sadistic killers partnered up. That will mean trouble."

"How many agents will remain here?"

"My team and I will remain here as long as needed. When Thorguson and his accomplice move to another town, a smaller team will stay here to assist you with the investigation. I am determined to bring these men in."

Bankston was relieved. "If you need anything at all, don't hesitate to ask. I'll call a local motel and make arrangements for you and your team."

"Thank you, we appreciate it."

"Would you like to see the bodies? I am sure the coroner is still there."

"If possible, that would be beneficial," O'Riordan replied.

Bankston called Dr. Welsh. "Doc, I have some FBI agents from the Behavioral Analysis Unit here. Would it be possible for us to come over and inspect the bodies of the couple that we found?"

"How long before you'll get here?"

"We can be there in about twenty minutes."

"That's fine. It will give me time to finish up with the latest autopsy before you arrive. Any idea why the Feds are here?"

"The dead couple may be linked to a serial killer, or killers. The FBI is chasing them down."

"I'll give them a rundown on my findings when they get here."

"Thanks Doc. See you soon."

***

Dr. Welsh had just finished up, when Bankston and O'Riordan arrived. "Dr. Welsh, this is Special Agent Jackson O'Riordan. He is in charge of the task force in search of David Thorguson, the serial killer that escaped from Hope, Louisiana."

O'Riordan shook Dr. Welsh's hand. "Dr. Welsh, thank you for fitting me in." Extending his arm towards Dr. Cook, "And this is a fellow colleague."

Meghan stepped forward, "Dr. Welsh, my name is Dr. Meghan Cook. I am a coroner with the State of Mississippi."

"Pleased to meet you both." He brought them over to the gurney and pulled back the sheet. "I don't have the full autopsy report ready just yet, and still no results on toxicology."

"That's okay, Dr. Welsh. I'm not worried about the toxicology results as much as the way they were murdered. The serial killer I am chasing has a specific signature."

"Well, I can let you know that the bodies both had super glue applied to their sexual orifices and anuses. The torture and mutilation on the bodies was overkill, if you ask me."

Agent O'Riordan looked over the bodies and had to agree. "This fits the pattern of the MO and signature I've been researching. The good news for you, Detective Bankston, is this duo only kills once per city. They have probably moved on, which means I need to find out where they are headed to next."

Dr. Welsh informed O'Riordan, "Most of the stab wounds were superficial. The killers revived the victims several times before they were killed. Several ribs were fractured and petechial hemorrhage was evident, but exsanguination also took place. The bastards took their time with the victims."

"David Thorguson enjoys extending the torture on his victims as long as he can. From what I've researched on his accomplice, he also prefers to torture his victims for as long as possible. Now that these two partnered up, there is no telling what may happen, but it won't be anything good."

Neither killer cared that he was leaving behind fingerprints or DNA. It was as if he wanted to taunt them, 'Look where I've been and what I've done'.

***

O'Riordan and his team inspected the crime scene as well. Sometimes clues were overlooked and it took a second set of eyes to notice them. They spent hours working under the sun, repeatedly walking the scene to ensure nothing, no fibers, fingerprints, hair, had been missed. The scene was thoroughly photographed. The local crime scene techs had done a meticulous job. O'Riordan asked that the evidence be sent to the FBI labs and a rush was ordered. Unfortunately, it could take weeks for all the physical evidence to be examined.

Sitting around a table at a local restaurant, discussing their findings, Dr. Meghan Cook quickly spoke up, "Rohypnol is an older drug. With so many new drugs out there, I think this has to be an older man. He has to be good looking to get close enough to slip these women a roofie in their drinks."

O'Riordan agreed. "I think he is in his late 30's to early 40's. One reason he may use Rohypnol is the cost, as well. Nowadays, it is cheap. With the way he moves around, he either must conserve his money or has an abundance of it.

"We are mapping out the areas he has been. We have areas where the victims may have been abducted differentiated from where the bodies were discovered. This may help us ascertain where they are headed to next."

Meghan asked, "Have all the victims been identified?"

O'Riordan frowned, "No, some victims haven't been identified. We are searching through missing person's reports to see if we may obtain a match that way. I have an agent contacting family members of those we suspect are potential victims for anything that can possibly give us a DNA profile. Another agent is also working on a computer program to sort the DNA and match the missing person and unidentified body."

Bankston asked, "Do you have any suspects at all?"

"No, we have no idea who is working with Thorguson. His fingerprints and DNA are not in CODIS or any other database. He has managed to stay completely off the grid."

***

Jordan saw the express mail package waiting for her. There had to be a reason he sent it express and she dreaded opening it. She walked around her desk and sat down, staring at the package for a few minutes.

She leaned over, picked up the phone, and dialed. "Alex, a package came via express mail. It is postmarked Raleigh, North Carolina. I am fairly certain it contains a body part."

"I am already on my way to meet you for lunch. I'll be there in a second."

Thankfully it didn't take Alex long to get there. As he walked over to her, she thrust the package in his hands. Inside the package, he found two pairs of ears, perfectly severed from their victims.

Alex immediately took his phone out of his shirt pocket and hit speed dial for O'Riordan's number. "O'Riordan, I have your victims' ears. He sent them to Jordan."

Alex despised the fact that David kept sending Jordan mementoes of his kills, but at least by him doing this, they could keep track of this duo. "What did the note say?"

"I forgot how much fun it was with two."

Chapter 12

Stan and Tori Donovans' memorial was today. Agent O'Riordan felt an obligation to make an appearance.

The evening matched the somber occasion. The sky was gray and it appeared as if in any minute the heavens would open up and let the rain out. Agent O'Riordan found a place in the back, not wanting to disturb the family. He listened intently, as the minister spoke of the Donovans and their love for each other and their families.

The Donovans would spend their eternal rest in an elaborate mausoleum in the cemetery. Several mausoleums, marble gravestones, stone angels, and cherubs graced the cemetery, some dating back to the civil war. It was a peaceful place to be laid to rest. Agent O'Riordan felt a deep sympathy for their families, as the minister spoke the final words, "Ashes to ashes, dust to dust…" Tori Donovan's mother was beside herself with grief and regrettably, there were no words of comfort he could offer her. These poor souls wouldn't be able to rest until their murderers were brought to justice. "On Angels Wings" played as the coffins were placed into the mausoleum. O'Riordan slipped away before the family was ready to depart.

O'Riordan heard his name being called and turned around. Stan Donovan's dad was walking towards him, "Agent, please catch this bastard for us."

"Yes sir, I am planning on it."

* * *

Dean Albright had been keeping track of Agent O'Riordan's moves. He must think the Donovans' deaths had something to do with Thorguson and his accomplice or he wouldn't be here. If the FBI had linked any murders to the men, they hadn't released any of the information. Albright wasn't sure who the woman was with O'Riordan, but he intended to find out.

Albright took a quick nip of the Maker's Mark whiskey he kept in his flask, just for fortification. He felt the delicious warmth of the liquor make its way down his throat. This had been one of those days where he needed to feel something. The day was rainy and plain gloomy, fitting weather for a funeral.

Albright had kept his distance, watching from his Lexus. He didn't want O'Riordan to know he was following him, or he would attempt to put a gag order on him. Albright had his sources and had also been keeping up with unsolved murders. If his research was correct, this story would be bigger than just Thorguson escaping from prison. Albright had heard rumors that O'Riordan was becoming obsessed with this case and capturing this duo. If only Albright could get near O'Riordan and ask him if he suspected that there was another serial killer out there with Thorguson, one who was just as depraved as him.

Albright suspected that he may be onto a case big enough for a book. Something that might land him on the coveted bestseller list. He needed to get all his facts straight. He was willing to do anything for this story. He started his car as O'Riordan and his date drove off.

***

When they left the funeral, it was late afternoon and the sun had started to set. Meghan kept quiet on the way back to the hotel. Neither one of them was hungry, the grimness of the day wore heavy on their hearts. The families of the deceased had been inconsolable. Meghan studied O'Riordan's profile.

Meghan could tell the Donovans' funeral had upset him more than he wanted to admit. She took his hand in hers and squeezed. He kissed her hand and said, "Thank you for accompanying me today."

"I wanted to be here for you. You know, this isn't your fault. There is no way you could have ever predicted any of this."

"If only I had pursued this killer when I first became aware of his signature."

"O'Riordan, it wasn't your call. You just had suspicions and not hard evidence."

"It bothers me that even after all this time; with all these murders, no one has a description of this killer. This man has made no mistakes, left no clues behind - even after helping Thorguson escape. It's like he is a ghost. How does he stay so well hidden and where the hell are they headed to next?

"He has lived a gypsy lifestyle as far as I can tell. He has to pick up odd jobs to survive, but how does he find the work? We know he drives a motor home, so it must be insured, but how? Unless he has gotten lucky all these years, without being stopped for not having plates. He may even steal plates on similar motor homes and swap as needed."

***

Meghan wanted to help O'Riordan forget about today's funerals, and take a breather from the case for a brief moment in time. After leaving the funeral she had tried to ease the tension by inviting him inside for a drink, but the man was focused on finding the killer. But she feared that if he didn't relieve some of the tension building up inside of him he would have a heart attack. Since she couldn't convince him to stay the night, there was only one thing to do – go to him. By the time she had made it to the hotel, O'Riordan was getting settled into his hotel room.

She impatiently knocked on his door. She greeted him with a passionate kiss and pushed his suit jacket off of him, where it dropped to the floor with a thud. She loosened his tie next, never breaking her kiss. She didn't want to give him the chance to say no. His hands moved up and started to massage her breasts, teasing her nipples. Her clothes pooled at her feet as he lifted her up and carried her to the bed.

"I want you so bad, O'Riordan. I can't wait." She felt like molten lava, desire flickered in her eyes. Meghan ran her hands up and down his body, enjoying the way his sinewy muscles felt. He tilted her face up to his one more time, kissing her with such passion. His touch explored, sending goose bumps up and down her skin. His erection pressed into her body. She stroked him, already wild with need for him. She was already wet and ready for him; her very core throbbed to feel him inside her.

She moaned when he took her breast into his mouth. "Jackson, please, I need you."

He continued trailing hot kisses down her body, sending erotic sensations through her very being. The light stubble of his beard was more than she could take; it sent an erotic shock straight to her core. She ran her hands through his hair, clinging to him. "O'Riordan, please." He entered her in one swift movement. She opened herself wider for him, taking all of him. She wanted to be one with him, completely.

The hot friction of him moving inside her was pure, sweet torture. Each thrust brought her closer to orgasm. She lifted herself up higher to him, feeling him plunge even deeper inside her. Jackson's thrusts grew faster, more urgent. Fireworks exploded inside her, as she climaxed. Her body tightened around his erection. She heard Jackson cry out as he found his own release. Afterwards, neither one wanted to move, enjoying being in each other's embrace.

****

O'Riordan needed to take a step away from the case and come back the next day with a clear head. He had been working without a break and thought of nothing except the case, even in his sleep. Even Meghan had been trying to get him to think of something else for a brief period of time.

Meghan was the one good thing about this case. He couldn't picture his life without her. Once this case was over, they would go their separate ways, but he didn't want to think about that right now. Maybe after all was said and done, they could work something out.

Right now, he had a couple of serial killers to find and until they were behind bars, he couldn't afford to take time off. Besides, he despised days off. He ran and worked out, but that was to stay in shape. Running was his stress relief in the morning.

Hell, he didn't even own a house, just a small furnished apartment. Why waste the money, when he was never there? He seemed to always be on the road, chasing one psychopath after another. They never stopped coming; it never ended.

Chapter 13

The eagerness had reached a feverish peak. The Hunter had talked nonstop about it the past two days. Since he freed The Hunter, the need had been voracious. Killing too often would eventually make the FBI aware of his activities and he didn't want that. He had been so careful over the years to keep his existence from surfacing, but his appetite had become never ending. He could no longer fight the urge to kill.

"It is time to hunt. Nightfall is fast approaching."

"Let's go hunting, my friend."

The Traveler let the cigarette smoke slowly leave his mouth and nose, while he waited and watched for his next victim. He was propped up against a tree near the women's restrooms at the rest stop. The Hunter had requested a woman this time.

The night sky was a shimmering mass of twinkling stars. The full moon cast a soft glow across the picturesque grounds of the rest stop. The Traveler took another thorough look to confirm that he hadn't missed a security camera. He didn't want his face caught on camera.

The Traveler spotted the Camaro pulling in and perked up. He took another long, hard drag of his cigarette and waited.

He saw the girl as soon as she exited the vehicle. She wore a tight pair of blue jeans and black turtleneck. The Traveler watched in awe as she walked in the high heel boots with ease. Her dark hair flowed behind her as she strode to the restroom in a hurry. She had a perky little bounce to her walk. She moved with a confidence that he couldn't wait to break.

***

Harley Allen exited her Camaro and took a deep breath. Freedom, that's what she smelled in the air, glorious freedom. She finally did it. She left that hell hole she had called home for eighteen years. When she opened her mail this morning and saw the acceptance letter to Virginia State, she couldn't believe it, a full scholarship, including dorm. She grabbed what meager belongings she had and took off, never looking back. She didn't even bother to inform her parents, they wouldn't miss her anyhow.

This was the beginning of her new life. She no longer feared being stuck in that small town, living under her parents' roof. She had been given the chance to improve herself, make something of her life. Best of all, she was embarking on this journey where no one knew her past, where she came from or anything else about her.

Good times in Harley's childhood had been few and far between. Early on she had learned to savor the fleeting and rare special moments, knowing it would be quite some time before something good may happen again. By the time Harley entered high school, she had learned that dreams and wishes were for fools. If you wanted something in this world, you had to make it happen. She had always been a guarded person. Trust didn't come easy to her, she let few people inside her circle. If you ever betrayed that trust, she would write you out of her life. She saw everything in black and white, there was no gray.

Maybe her luck was about to change, though. Her dad was still passed out drunk on his recliner when she left. She doubted her mom would even know she was gone. She didn't care if she had to live in her car until school started in the fall; she was out of that miserable place.

Harley never saw the man emerging from the shadows. He yanked her head back as he placed his arm around her neck. She felt his hand cover her mouth and nose. Something in his hand smelled cloyingly sweet.

Her heart hammered in fear. Her mind was reeling; what was happening? This couldn't possibly be happening to her. She struggled to free herself.

Tears burned her eyes, but she refused to let them flow. She tried not to breath in whatever drug he had doused on the rag. Trepidation started to take over, replacing every sensation in her body. She kicked and twisted as she tried frantically to free herself from this maniac's grip. However, the drug made her dazed. As the drug took over, she lost her battle to stay conscious. Soon, oblivion wrapped her in its cold embrace.

***

Harley awakened slowly, as the fog cleared from her brain. Her eyelids felt as if weights were attached to them and her mouth felt as if someone had stuffed it full of cotton. Her arms and feet were secured to a bed. She was lying spread eagle and naked. She tried to pull on the restraints, but they were too tight.

Now that her vision had cleared, she found herself in a small, stark room. All around her was nothing but a deafening, eerie silence. She yanked on the restraints one more time, but they refused to budge. All she managed to accomplish was to cut into her wrists and ankles.

Harley was confused. Where was she? With every little movement, pain zipped right through her. It cut her right to the bone. Through the darkness and the fog of her memory she struggled to remember what happened to her. Her insides were on fire, it hurt to breath. The last thing she remembered was pulling into a rest stop.

A door opened and sunlight came streaming in, blinding her momentarily. Crap, how long had she been out? It was nighttime when she pulled into a rest stop.

When the man entered the room, she would never have speculated that evil could be so handsome. Evil should be menacing, a repugnant monster. She now knew that evil could take on the look of many, many faces. It wasn't always apparent when looking at someone, to know what lived inside their soul.

"Please, don't hurt me." Harley saw the knife in his hand and panicked. "What are you going to do to me?"

The Traveler let out an ominous chuckle. "Me? Don't you mean us? I have a comrade here to help me. He became quite enraptured with your beauty while you were unconscious. He couldn't wait for you to wake up and had some fun already."

Harley had had some appalling things happen to her in the past, but nothing like this. This made being beat by her drunken dad seem like child's play. Nausea washed over her as she tried to move. Her limbs quivered from being in their position for so long.

Maybe Harley's dad had been right and she was a bad girl. After all, killers flocked to the bad girls in the movies. Every time her dad beat her he told her she brought it upon herself, that it was her fault and she had to be punished. What did she do to deserve to be punished like this?

She felt hopelessness rising up, threatening to overtake her. Something snapped inside of Harley, she refused to show her captors fear. She did not bring this upon herself. It was not her fault that someone abducted her. If she had any hopes of survival, she must show some backbone.

She felt the man's hands wrapping around her neck, squeezing the life out of her. It would be so easy to close her eyes and let death take her away. Let the darkness wash over her, taking away all the years of pain. A primal instinct bubbled up inside of her, the fight to live conquers the desire to give up and die. She wanted to live. She was starting a new life. She'd finally moved out of her parents' house and was ready to find herself.

She opened her eyes and stared into the eyes of the man strangling her. If he did kill her, she wanted her image to be the last thing he saw when he closed his eyes. She looked up at her abductor and returned his icy, emotionless stare. Looking into his eyes, she saw something that sent a shiver down her spine. In that instant, she knew she was looking into the eyes of a maniacal killer. Pure evil stared back at her. She didn't back down from his glare. If he wanted to kill her now and end this, he would have to do it with her looking back at him.

The pain became all consuming. She allowed the pain to help keep her focused. Somehow, she had to escape. She knew his kind. They got off on fear and control. He may have the upper hand right now, but she refused to show fear. It was time to show gumption and fight back.

"You don't scare me. You think you can do worse than what others before you have done to me? As if." She knew she was goading him on, but so be it. If he killed her, it wouldn't be because she was docile and gave in to fear.

Vehemence flowed through The Traveler as he raised his hand and slapped her hard across the face. Pain pulsed across her face. She saw stars when he connected with her face.

She just laughed at him. "Is that the best you got?" When she spoke, her voice never faltered, no hint of the terror she felt could be heard. Even when she caught a glimpse of the other man walking towards her. That one was truly diabolical. Even the devil himself was probably petrified of him.

The Hunter handed his friend a filet knife. "Have you ever fileted a fish? It's quite effortless you know. I've always wondered what it would be like to slowly filet a living person. Would you like to help me?"

"I haven't slaughtered anything in quite some time. This could get messy. We need to cover the room in sheets, just in case we have more than a little blood splatter."

When the darkness came to take her away, she visualized her soul leaving her body and drifting away. Harley did not fear death any longer.

***

Officers Harry Percle and Jacob Elroy responded to the call from dispatch regarding an abandoned vehicle at a rest stop off of I-95. The concierge noticed it when she arrived at work that morning. She had been observing the comings and goings of visitors and no one had approached it. She sent a security guard to check the restrooms and they were empty.

Officer Percle turned to his partner, "What does your gut say? Registration is for an eighteen year old girl. The parents didn't even know she was missing. The dispatcher said the father sounded drunk."

"She is most probably a runaway."

"Yeah, but where is she?"

"Maybe she met up with a boyfriend, who knows. There doesn't seem to be any signs of foul play."

"Let's call in for a tow truck and at least send out a BOLO for her. Other than that, there isn't much we can do."

Chapter 14

Park Ranger Ken Sutherland winced as the scalding hot coffee hit his tongue. At one time, he enjoyed coming into work, but lately it had become monotonous. Nothing exciting ever happened, and worse yet, very few campers had been around. He decided to start his morning rounds early to fight off boredom.

At one time, this had been a popular camping spot. As the years passed, camping lost its appeal to most families. What with resorts and hotels with swimming pools popping up along the interstate, camping had lost its allure to the masses.

The park had begun to show years of disrepair, but at least the scenery remained breathtaking. From this particular spot, you could catch a glimpse of the lake. The wharf around the lake had seen its better days. It looked as if a good wind would blow it away. Most of the buildings around here were falling apart. If only they had the budget for a few minor renovations. Ken always enjoyed camping in the Boy Scouts, which was one of the main reasons he choose this profession.

A group of buzzards were flocking at a campsite in the back. Curiosity got the best of him and he decided to see what had died. If a bear mauled something, he had to warn campers of the potential danger.

***

Detective Sam Morrison pulled up at the crime scene and parked his car behind the other patrol cars. There were more cars out here than he'd anticipated. It must be worse than he initially thought. He adjusted his holster and turned his phone to vibrate. Now he wished he had grabbed a quick cup of coffee.

Looking around the campground, he noticed that fall was fast approaching. Leaves showed vibrant hues of yellow, orange, and red. Even the temperatures had dropped in the low double digits. Maybe the mosquitoes wouldn't be as prevalent as normal and the crime scene could be worked without getting eaten alive by the blasted things.

The coroner, Dr. Adam Richardson, had somehow managed to beat him here once again. Hell, his partner, Detective Blake Sotheby, even arrived before him. "About time you made it. What's wrong Pops? That new baby keeping you up all night?"

Morrison smiled. "It's worth it, though. She is a gorgeous little baby." This was Doreen's and his first child and they were ecstatic with her birth. Shelby Lynn had become the light of his life.

The coroner was walking their way, "How's the new baby?"

"She's great. Already a Daddy's girl."

"That's great! Well, you have yourself a doozy of a case here. It's bad, it looks as if she was skinned alive."

They all moved to the crime scene. Sunlight filtered through the trees, as they walked through the woods. Before entering the actual crime scene they suited up, putting on their booties and gloves. One of the techs was already snapping pictures like a pro. Jenkins, who was collecting evidence, looked up briefly and gave a quick acknowledgement. A good deal of time would be spent taking pictures and documenting the crime scene. Even with decomp, it appeared that the victim was a young female. At least he assumed they were dealing with a female. Both breasts had been removed, as well as most of her skin. A mane of long auburn hair hid her face at the moment.

With the degree of decomposition, identification wouldn't be easy. Surely someone had filed a missing person's report on her. Someone so young had to be missed, a parent waiting for her to come home or a boyfriend wondering where she was. They were dealing with a sick son of a bitch. Even after death, it appeared as though her body had been violated.

Morrison observed the surroundings. "I don't notice any blood around the body or the surrounding area."

Sotheby agreed, "No, I don't think she was killed here. It looks like a body dump. The park ranger did say he had one motor home check in earlier this week and checked out two days ago. We are running plates now. Unfortunately, payment is made in a drop box and the campers write down their own information. I'm willing to bet he didn't provide any legit information to go on. The park ranger isn't even sure of an exact description of the motor home. If it hadn't been for the buzzards circling, we might not have found the body for weeks."

The coroner brought their attention to the victim's neck, "It appears as if she was strangled. There are also lash marks, possibly from a whip, several stab wounds and burn marks. What's even more disturbing is that I found she has been eviscerated. We noticed it when we straightened her body. I won't know for sure until autopsy, but it looks like several organs may have been removed."

"Any other observations?" Morrison reckoned this would be an unusual murder case they had on their hands.

"There are definite ligature marks on her arms and legs."

"What about ID? Did anyone spot a purse or wallet around the site?"

"Nothing has turned up so far."

"So doc, do you see any birthmarks or tattoos?"

"I can't say for sure, but it looks like any identifying marks were removed when she was skinned. This poor girl was put through hell."

"Looks like we may be dealing with a pro. Let's search VICAP, we may get a hit." Turning to another officer, Morrison stated, "We need to identify her. Check out missing persons for the last few weeks and see what they have."

Sotheby looked over the body and said, "We need to bag her hands; maybe she fought back before he restrained her. Any signs of sexual assault doc?"

"I won't know until the autopsy. It looks like he used super glue on her. That's a new one for me. I'll do the autopsy at 4:00 this afternoon, if you all want to drop by."

Morrison wondered if she knew her killer. Murder often happened when love went bad for some unfortunate women. Love had been known to turn vicious at times. Lovers, husbands, or boyfriends spurned could turn violent in the blink of an eye. The skinning, evisceration and the super glue, though, made him lean towards someone with experience having perpetrated this murder. It seemed like such overkill on the body.

With decomposition so bad on their Jane Doe, Detective Morrison requested that a sketch artist go over to the morgue to look at her bone structure.

Hopefully the artist could piece together a sketch of the girl that they could broadcast to the public, asking for help identifying her.

***

Morrison and Sotheby arrived at the coroner's office a few minutes before 4:00. It took longer at the crime scene than they initially thought. There was a lot of ground to cover and they found several distinct tire impressions. As they pushed the large double metal doors open, the smell of bleach and cleaners overwhelmed their senses. Morrison despised this part of his job. He had never been squeamish about blood, but the sounds of the tools used in here tended to give him the creeps.

Dr. Richardson and his assistant were ready to begin. The body lay in front of them on a stainless steel gurney. Morrison secretly hoped Dr. Richardson had already managed to make the y-incision beforehand.

As the detectives donned their scrubs, booties, and gloves, Morrison stiffened, as he spied the table of saws and other instruments. It was such a gruesome little collection in his mind. Dr. Richardson pulled back the sheet that covered the woman, "Let's begin, gentlemen."

They listened as the doctor did a thorough external exam. Numerous stab and burn wounds were noted, as well as the strangulation and ligature marks. When he moved down to the pelvic region, he remarked, "Her vaginal and anal areas were sealed with super glue. From the bruising around her genitalia, I can say with certainty that she was sadistically sexually assaulted beforehand. If this killer has struck before, this may indeed give you a clue to his victims. I will check with some fellow coroners to see if they've had any victims present with the same type of injuries."

Morrison and Sotheby both agreed that was an excellent idea. Not all law enforcement agencies ran the cases through VICAP, but a coroner would remember certain details like super glue.

"Looks like we may have some DNA detectives. Semen is present. He didn't bother to wash her down, so either he doesn't care, or is a newbie. It will take approximately a week to get the results, but when we do receive the results, they can be run through CODIS." CODIS is a national database of DNA collected from the convicted, missing persons and unsolved cases. "I was able to lift several prints off of her body and those are being run through AFIS right now."

Dr. Richardson stated, "I had Tim rush the toxicology report for me. A presumptive report was sent over this morning. Chloroform was used to subdue her. Trace amounts were found in her system."

Morrison was astounded to hear that. "Chloroform? That is old school, isn't it?"

"There are more options out there, but chloroform is easy to acquire. He must be familiar with it, though, because there is a danger in using it. If you aren't careful, you can breathe it in and knock yourself out."

Morrison wouldn't be able to forget this girl's face for a long time. It would haunt his dreams until he solved this case. The girl's eyes were open and bulging. Petechial hemorrhaging and massive bruising was evident on her body, especially on her neck. From the hideous expression on her face, it was apparent she died a horrendous death. Patches of skin had been removed from her body. Most startling was that this girl had been skinned alive. Bite marks were also present all over the body. What had been done to her was unfathomable. You could see every horrific thing this maniac did to her.

Morrison couldn't even begin to conceive the horrors this girl went through. "I want video and stills taken of the body. I will send a copy to VICAP and the FBI immediately. I think Dr. Richardson is correct in his assumption. This is not the first time this killer has struck."

What kind of person would do this to another human being? What kind of twisted mind did this person have to even contemplate these tortures on another person?

With the external exam done, Dr. Richardson was ready to continue on to the y-incision. Morrison didn't need to be around for this violation of the body. It may be a necessary evil to solve the case, but the woman had already been through enough, without needing them to witness the rest. "Doc, we will let you finish up here. There are still some leads we need to follow up on."

"I'll send you my report when it's complete."

The killer or killers had spent a great deal of time with the victim, never feeling the need to hurry along. They knew what they were doing. No, this wasn't a newbie to killing. This was someone experienced.

Morrison drove back to the Sheriff's Department in silence. The building was over fifty years old and needed minor renovations. When it was originally constructed, someone had the foresight to keep in mind the town would grow and as it did, a bigger building would be needed. There were more than enough offices to house all the detectives and give them a little more growing room for labs, interview rooms, and conference rooms.

***

Morrison noticed the FBI agent as soon as he walked into the station. His black suit and the presence about him screamed FBI. It couldn't be a coincidence that he arrived right after a brutal murder here.

O'Riordan walked up to the sergeant at the front desk, "I'm looking for a Detective Morrison."

Morrison had just made it to the desk when he heard his name. "That's me. What can I do for you, Agent?"

O'Riordan was astonished that he had been pegged as FBI so quickly. "I am with the BAU. You entered a case into VICAP yesterday about a murder involving super glue. I wanted to talk to you about it, if at all possible."

"Let's go back to my desk. I haven't had a chance to check on the hits from VICAP yet. You must have been watching for new cases. I had a feeling this wasn't just a garden variety murder. I assume the FBI suspects my murder may be that of a serial killer or madman they are currently hunting down."

"I have an alert set up that notifies me as soon as something matching my request is entered. I also noticed that you mentioned the body was eviscerated. The evisceration is new, but the super glue does match my killer. I'm fairly certain this is his work."

"To be honest with you, when I saw the body, I thought it was the work of a pro. The body is in decomp and scavengers managed to do a number on her, but you can still tell that the torture she endured was excruciating."

"I am in charge of the task force that is tracking down an escaped serial killer, David Thorguson, and his partner. Now that these two have teamed up, I have been worried the brutality done to the victims would become worse. The violence is clearly escalating. Unfortunately, we don't know much about his partner, the one who helped him escape."

"Whatever you need, just let me know. I am a firm believer that we, as law enforcement agencies, need to all get along. What this girl endured was inhumane."

"I appreciate it, Detective Morrison. I made a copy of my relevant files for your perusal, if you're interested. Maybe if we all work together, we can bring this duo down."

Morrison picked up the file and looked over the photos. "Except for the skinning and evisceration, you would assume we were looking at the same crime scene."

O'Riordan handed over the photos of the crime scenes before David became involved with his partner. "Now, I want you to take a look at these."

"They are close, but not nearly as macabre as the recent crime scenes."

"These are the work of a possible serial killer that has managed to fly under the radar. I stumbled across the similarities by accident quite some time ago. I, however, never really had the proof and the powers that be felt I would be spinning my wheels and wasting federal funds when the FBI already had a heavy caseload. After David Thorguson escaped and the prison guard had the same signature, I was given a chance to prove my theory."

"These were all the work of your suspected serial killer?"

"We still don't know for sure if all these cases are related. They all have similarities, but, yes, I do believe most were committed by the same killer. It appears that this killer knew by crossing state lines it would keep him from being discovered. He never seems to strike the same area twice. He also keeps his victimology different."

"I noticed there are both men and women victims."

"I don't think the killings are sexually motivated for him. It's all about the control and torture. The amount of pain he can inflict while ending a life is what his killings seem to revolve around. With him, it's a matter of opportunity. This killer isn't going for a particular look, anyone will do."

Morrison continued reviewing the files. Each of these victims had died a horrible, gruesome death. The coroners had been thorough with the autopsies. Every clue or chance for DNA that could be considered was explored. DNA had been found in some cases, but with no hits. For some unknown reason, the DNA hits never linked the murders, even though after reviewing some of the files, the matches were there.

"Why didn't VICAP pick up on the DNA matches?"

O'Riordan had wondered the same thing when he noticed the matches. "There was a glitch somewhere, but one that I am rectifying with this case."

Looking at Morrison, O'Riordan could tell the man had a tremendous amount of empathy for the victims. He was very thorough in his investigations, from what he had observed. "We could use someone like you on the task force. At each sighting, I keep a small task force there to continue working the case. We all touch base as the case progresses. Some travel may be needed, though. If you are interested, I can speak with your lieutenant and have you temporarily assigned to the case."

Morrison was taken aback by the request. This could be a huge help in his career - or it could ruin him. Some of his fellow officers in the department considered working with the FBI as a weakness. These monsters needed to be stopped, though, and if "sleeping with the enemy", as they saw it, was the only way to do that, then so be it. Although he never considered the FBI to be the enemy.

"Agent O'Riordan, I'll do anything I can to help capture these bastards. If you need a place to set up here, I'm sure we can find some empty offices. Anything you or the task force need, don't hesitate to ask. We had a kidnapping case not long ago and there are already extra phone lines set up, as well as whiteboards."

"I'm sure your coroner here is just as good as the one we have on the task force, but would it be okay for her to examine the body?"

"I have no problems with it and I don't see where the coroner will either."

***

As Meghan walked into the morgue, she prayed the coroner wouldn't be hostile and hold this request against her. Dr. Richardson walked over to her with a file in his hands. She didn't sense any hostility in his mannerism. "You must be Dr. Cook, it's nice to meet you. I made you a copy of the autopsy report. We still don't have any lab results back, regrettably. This is a hell of a case."

"It's a pleasure to meet you. I hope you didn't take any offense at the FBI's request."

"Doesn't bother me one bit. I'm confident in my work and if I did miss something, and I don't believe I did, then we need to know about it."

"I honestly don't think Agent O'Riordan is worried that you missed anything, it's just that I've been reviewing these files over and over lately and I believe I have picked up on his signature. If that's the case, it won't take but a quick perusal of the body to know for certain."

"I have her ready for you to look at. We still don't have an ID yet."

Meghan donned her scrubs, booties, and gloves. She examined the young woman's body, taking blood and tissue samples to expedite to the FBI lab for results. She shook her head. This was such a waste of a young life. The body was a disaster. Numerous cuts, stab wounds, burns, and bruises covered her body. The killers had started to take their torture further.

She must rein in these emotions and channel them to her benefit. She needed to be methodical, but also proceed with haste in this case. The longer these two killers were free, the more bodies would be found. Agent O'Riordan joined them in the morgue.

"Agent O'Riordan, as I told Dr. Cook, I am confident in my work and we all have the same goal in mind – to catch this killer. Maybe with the federal government's resources, her identity can be located and her family informed of her unfortunate demise."

"He's escalating. The evisceration is new."

As Meghan continued to examine the body, she stated, "From the broken ribs and ligature marks around her neck, I suspect that they would revive her and start all over again."

O'Riordan nodded in agreement. "That is something David Thorguson would do. He revived them as many times as he could."

This duo was playing a dangerous cat and mouse game. Unfortunately, one never knew what went on in the mind of a diabolical killer, or in this case, killers.

Chapter 15

Sheriff Hamilton saw the envelope on her desk when she returned from lunch. Memories from the past came rushing back to her. She knew David was into psychological torture, as well as physical. For some insane reason, he felt the need to contact her. Even though she had not opened it yet, she knew it was from him. This could only mean he had struck again.

"Alex, I received another delivery today. This time it's an envelope so maybe he just sent a note. The postmark is from Smithfield, Virginia."

"Jordan, I want to be there when you open it. I'll be there shortly."

Jordan prayed that it was just a note this time. At least now they knew he was in Virginia, but where the hell was he going. For someone who had no money, he did an extensive amount of traveling. Where in the hell was he getting his money from and where were they staying? She had a hard time picturing Thorguson living in a motor home, but that was the only plausible explanation. The evidence so far pointed to this conclusion.

On his way into the office, Alex gave O'Riordan a call. "Jordan got another note from David today. I asked her not to open it until I get there."

"I'll have someone from the task force come and get it. The postmark wouldn't by chance be from anywhere in Virginia would it?"

"Smithfield, Virginia to be exact. Why, what happened?"

"Damn, I'm betting he's sending her tokens from his latest kill. A young girl was recently found mutilated here in Virginia. Not only was she eviscerated, but she was skinned alive."

"O'Riordan, he's escalating. He still has a fascination with Jordan too. I don't like this one bit."

Alex arrived at Jordans' office and opened the envelope.

Alex read the note, "Have you ever wondered what the inside of your body looks like? It is really fascinating to peek underneath the skin." David had included a few bloody fingernails with the note.

Jordan asked, "He's escalating, isn't he?"

"He is. This one was bad, I'm sorry."

"Where the hell are they going? Is he aimlessly traveling across the country?"

"Unfortunately, they might be. That is part of his accomplice's MO."

***

O'Riordan knew after the latest murder, the task force needed to meet again and strategize. They were getting nowhere and had to rethink their plan of attack. There had to be some way to figure out where the killers were going. Somehow, someway they were finding money to help them survive on the road. O'Riordan knew for a fact that Thorguson had not tried to obtain any funds from his bank. The FBI had asked the bank to reactivate all Thorguson's accounts just in case he did try, that way a trace could be made. That was wishful thinking, though. So far, no attempt had been made.

The killings were sadistic; no mercy had been shown on any victim they encountered. They lived for the thrill of the kill, to cause pain and suffering on those who were captured in their web. The killings weren't about jealousy or revenge, not even crimes of passion, but about power and control. They lived to inflict fear and pain. With the increase of victims, O'Riordan knew that more would take place soon. He suspected that David's accomplice was learning some of David's tricks of the trade, so to speak, and enjoying the rush he received. To some killers, the kill was an adrenaline rush, just like a drug was to a junkie.

Agents O'Riordan and Manning, Dr. Meghan Cook, Alex Hamilton, the deputies, and other agents involved in the task force that could take the time to meet back in Hope, Louisiana, met to strategize. If it hadn't been for

Sheriff Hamilton's condition, they would have met in Mississippi or North Carolina. Since she had so much knowledge regarding David Thorguson, it was important that she be involved in the meeting. David had kept corresponding with her since his escape, so she may have more knowledge of his behavior than any of them. David Thorguson had his sights set on her since early on in the original investigation.

Even though Manning stayed behind in Hope, Louisiana to man the task force there, he had managed to keep everything updated. The timeline and photos were arranged on the board for their joint meeting. The timeline included an outline of the tokens David had sent Sheriff Hamilton, as well as where each was mailed from, helping map out where they had been.

"I believe we are looking for a male Caucasian, between thirty-five and forty years old. It is believed he has been torturing and killing men and women for several years now. His suspected signature is the use of super glue on the sexual orifices. The killings are not sexually motivated, but more about power and control. He has led a gypsy lifestyle, never holding down a career, or full time job for that matter. His main goal is to have enough cash on hand for the basic necessities in life. In order to obtain this, he may either steal or work odd jobs.

"Even though he is a loner, he has the ability to be charming and social. His charms may be superficial, but it is enough to allow him to get close to his victims. He is a highly organized individual and extremely neat, maybe bordering on obsessive compulsive tendencies. Before helping David escape, none of the bodies showed signs of sexual assault. Since David's escape, severe sexual assault has been noted on the female bodies, both anally and vaginally. The male victims have just shown horrendous torture.

"Both men enjoy playing god, dominating their captives. As with David, it is believed the unsub had someone dominate him during childhood, and now he feels the need to seek vengeance. He is proving to himself and others that he is the one in control, even if it is by force. With both men being alpha males, this can either be a devastating blow to what they thought would be a collaborative partnership, and cause severe turmoil in the ranks, or indeed make their partnership flourish and thrive. If their bond does grow stronger, then we are in serious trouble.

"I know without a doubt in my mind that David Thorguson's new found partner has been killing for years, maybe since his late teens or early adulthood. He has managed to fly under the radar for quite some time, traveling around the United States to keep from being detected. Some need lured him to help David Thorguson escape, and if we can figure out that need, that compulsion, we may be one step closer to capturing them and ending this nightmare.

"It might be that he kills or disposes of the bodies in small towns, knowing they don't have the resources available for a meticulous investigation, unless they invite the state or FBI in. Most law enforcement agencies don't waste too much time on the murder of high risk victims, unfortunately. When you throw in his transient behavior, it complicates the matter immensely."

Looking over the cases and photos, O'Riordan felt his belief in God slipping. He had never been a religious man, by any means, but he had always believed there was a God. This case was starting to give him serious doubts. He didn't want to lose his faith in God or man, but the depravity of these killers was horrendous. How could God create two human beings, almost exactly alike, that would harm other people in this way?

Chapter 16

David would remain in the motor home while his friend went hunting for a victim. The need to kill burned deep inside of David. He had a thirst that couldn't be quenched since he escaped. He had so much to catch up on.

The Traveler had his special little pills in his pocket to drug a potential victim. He wanted to please David with a prize catch.

The crowded bar would be the perfect hunting ground. There had to be over one hundred people dancing, drinking, and just mingling. Everyone seemed to have a partner tonight. The Traveler knew women looked at him and drooled. He had the athletic body and good looks to attract his victims, but he could also blend into his surroundings if he wanted to. He waited for the opportune moment and struck. None of his prey feared him in the beginning; it was when they woke up that they saw his true self.

***

Kelly Simpson had been looking forward to this night for days. She and her friends made plans earlier in the week to go bar hopping, pick up a hottie, and forget their worries for one night. So far, they had visited six clubs and she had yet to find someone to take her home. She was on the lookout for someone different from the normal guys that hung out in the bars around here.

As he walked around, he found the perfect woman. She had a voluptuous body. A smile stretched across his face. Yes, this one would definitely please David.

"Hi, mind if I sit down?"

Kelly looked up. She could get lost in this man's blue eyes. His body was sheer perfection, nice and tight. "Haven't seen you around here before. New in town?"

"Just passing through and looking for a good time."

"Well hun, you came to the right place."

"Can I buy you a drink?"

"Dirty martini."

"I'll be right back."

The Traveler walked up to the bar. "Bartender, dirty martini and a gin and tonic, please."

Kelly was glad the evening had picked up; she thought she would have to call it an early night. The man was definitely hot. He reminded her of a movie star, with his muscular arms and handsome face. She was betting the sex would be great with him.

"Want to dance?"

Kelly thought he would never ask. "I'd love to."

As soon as she stood up, the room started spinning. "On the other hand, maybe I should call it a night. I'm not feeling so good."

"Here, at least let me help you outside. What kind of car are you driving?"

Kelly attempted to answer him, but it was as if her mouth didn't want to cooperate. As he led her towards a motor home, she tried to tell him that it wasn't hers. Now her legs weren't cooperating and he had to drag her along. She saw the door open and heard men talking.

The Traveler's demeanor changed as soon as he walked into the motor home. Gone, was the charming man that Kelly met in the bar.

"About time you got back." David said impatiently.

"Patience, my friend. You mustn't worry; I found a special one just for you."

The Hunter looked over at his friend, "Have you ever wondered what the inside of a human body looks like? Lately, I've been wondering what makes the human body work the way it does. I say we need to explore human anatomy. You interested?"

"That might get messy in here."

"We can put plastic down. That should help make clean up easy. Afterwards, we can wrap the body in it and throw everything out." He'd experimented a little with the last one, but not nearly as much as he would have liked to. He looked down at the woman and admired her luscious body. She had such full, perfect breasts. Too bad he couldn't save them for a collection. He was hard as a rock with want and need. Anticipation burned through his loins. David knew he needed to get control of his desires or he would lose control. He couldn't wait to feel her blood on his body, feel her heartbeat cease, pulsing in his bare hands.

***

Kelly was having trouble waking up, if that wasn't bad enough, when she tried to sit up, she realized her body didn't want to follow her brain's simple commands. She must have had more to drink than she realized last night. She would have one hell of a hangover. Dread came over her when she noticed she still couldn't move. She feared that maybe someone slipped a roofie into her drink at the bar. Her eyes were wide open now. She was restrained, naked on a bed in a small room. Adrenaline rushed through her body, fear took over her senses.

Her mother had warned her about the dangers of picking up men in bars time and time again. Surely, a gorgeous creature like the one she wanted to hook up with last night wasn't evil. Only the crazed ones planned on hurting you. She tried to think back to last night, piecing together what happened. How did she end up in this mess?

As her eyes scanned the room, she saw two men watching her. She gave the man she didn't recognize a dark, brooding stare. "You better watch that stare, my sweet."

"What are you going to do about it? Obviously you can't get a woman with your looks, if you have to restrain me. What's wrong, you two can't get it up?" She knew she was goading them, but she refused to go down without a fight.

Fury raged through The Hunter and he grabbed a fistful of her hair and forced her to look at him. "Bitch, I will teach you a lesson. You will fear me before you die." He pressed the knife to her neck and watched as a bead of blood formed on the tip.

The Traveler reached for the knife. "My friend, it is too soon to kill her. We want to have fun first, am I right?"

The Hunter pulled the knife away from her neck and, instead, glided the knife down her cleavage, watching as the blood oozed from the shallow cut. She took in a deep breath from the sting of the wound.

"This is not your lucky day, guys. I refuse to give in to fear. I am ready to die, do with me what you will. I know I will go to heaven and you will go straight to hell."

The Hunter laughed in her face. "My dear, you are in Hell right now. One that I have created especially for trash like you."

As the smell of blood started to fill the room, she still refused to show the first signs of fear. She had a cockiness about her that neither man could break. She gave them a weak laugh, "What's wrong? Did a woman make you feel emasculated? Come on baby, untie me and I'll show you how a real man is supposed to fight."

Furious, The Hunter stated, "Don't you dare talk to me like that. Do you know who I am?"

"You are a pathetic, sissy of a man, who has to beat and torture a woman to make you feel like a real man." She might be playing a cat and mouse game, but she was ready for this to end. If she pissed him off bad enough, maybe he would kill her.

He dropped his gaze to her luscious breasts as he said, " I think it's time for you to see just how much of a man I am."

He rolled her onto her stomach and pinned her head to the bed. "You are a whore, and I am going to show you how a whore should be treated."

"You can take my body, but I will not bow down to you."

***

His resolve was on the edge. He was the one that held her life in his hands and she continued to taunt him. As he rammed into her, he reached around and grabbed her breast, squeezing the nipple until he heard a soft whimper escape from her mouth. She was all talk; he sensed the fear building in her. This caused him to grow harder. His tempo picked up even more, thrusting harder and harder. His erection throbbed even more with her growing whimpers. He grabbed a whip he kept nearby and increased his torture on her.

The Hunter heard The Traveler talking to him, breaking his rhythm. "My friend, I'm glad you are enjoying yourself, but let's not kill her just yet."

The Hunter set the whip down. "You are right, my friend. When I have had my release, we will begin the dissection."

He could feel her bravado slipping and terror building inside her. With each thrust, she tried to squirm away from him. She was screaming now. "No one can hear you scream. It's just the three of us and my friend isn't going to help you."

"Why are you doing this to me?"

The Hunter rolled her on her back. He wanted to look into her eyes and see the fear, with each thrust inside of her.

David laughed mockingly, he knew he had finally broken her.

***

The Traveler was proud of his decision to free The Hunter. The Hunter was turning out to be his one true friend, something he'd never had before. They both enjoyed talking about previous murders committed; sharing their passion without being condemned for it. He enjoyed the chance to share his hobby with someone else that embraced the same passion, truly understood the thrill.

The Traveler was also learning a lot from The Hunter. The Hunter taught him not to run from the impulses that drove him to kill, but to embrace them. Let them build up in him, until the need overcame him and then ride the wave.

The Traveler always thought of killing as a hobby. Now, after talking in depth with The Hunter, he knew it was a calling. It had taken root and become an addiction.

Chapter 17

Sheriff William Bradham enjoyed his job. Most people considered him to be a tough sheriff who showed no leniency to anyone. That may be true, but crime in this town had dropped significantly since his election. He was forty-two, single, and planned to keep it that way. Marriage and police work didn't mix. They were like oil and water.

Right before lunch, he received a call from Phil Jones, head of the local Department of Transportation office. "Sheriff Bradham, some men were removing trash from the roadside and stumbled across a dead body. It is near the entrance ramp to the interstate. I wasn't sure if this is your jurisdiction or the State Trooper's."

"Hard to say, give me the exact location and I'll give them a call. If it's a dead body, I have to call the state troopers in any way. They are better equipped to handle crime scenes." Sheriff Bradham hoped it was close to the interstate. He didn't want this kind of headache. He informed the state trooper dispatcher the location of the dead body.

The dispatcher asked, "Can you tell if foul play is involved?"

"I'm on my way out there now. We received the call a minute before I called you."

"I'll alert the local state trooper detachment near there."

"You may want to have them send out their crime scene unit. I'll dispatch mine, but our equipment is nowhere near as sophisticated as yours."

"Yes, sir, I'll let them know."

Sheriff Bradham called Detective Tony Morris and Detective Drew Powell into his office. "We have a dead body near the entrance ramp to the interstate. I informed the State Troopers, but we need to investigate, in case it turns out to be our jurisdiction. I'll be right behind you."

When they arrived, the men stepped out of their truck, but just pointed at the body. Neither man wanted to go near the body, much less take another look at it. "When we went to pick up the tarp, the hand fell out. We dropped the thing and called our supervisor."

Sheriff Bradham knew the men were just doing their job, but it also meant that the crime scene had inadvertently been tampered with. Both men would have to be fingerprinted, so their fingerprints could be separated from the killer's.

Sheriff Bradham informed his detectives. "Forensics and the coroner are on their way. It shouldn't be too much longer before they arrive. Our first priority is identifying the victim. Check for prints near and on the body. Maybe he left semen and the perp is in CODIS. Hell, you never know, we may get lucky and have this case wrapped up in forty-eight hours."

****

Detective Morris looked over the body while he waited for the coroner. Even in death, you could tell the young woman had been attractive. She was maybe twenty-five or so. From the looks of her bare feet, she'd recently had a pedicure. Her toenails were painted a bright fuchsia pink, once again indicating her young age. Perhaps if they brought her photo to local nail salons someone would recognize her. This girl must be missed by someone. After all, she was someone's daughter, sister, possibly a wife or girlfriend. Someone must have reported her missing.

Detectives Morris and Powell watched the coroner's van pull up. Both men wanted to be nearby while the coroner did a quick examination of the body. Upon examination, the coroner discovered that the victim had been eviscerated, but also her private parts appeared to be super glued shut. This gave the murder enough distinction to run the MO through VICAP and see if they found a hit. Hopefully, this would already be someone else's headache.

The mutilation and torture done to the body showed an extensive amount of rage. Multiple stab and burn marks covered the body.

Between the brutality of the crime scene and the heat, tempers started to wear thin. The men who discovered the body were getting restless, wondering when they could go home. Neither detective wanted to release them from the scene until forensics were done, just in case more questions needed to be answered. Besides, they wanted to ensure that neither man talked to the press just yet.

Morris observed his surroundings. He allowed the scene and evidence to tell its story. If he listened close enough, maybe some secrets would be revealed.

Crime scene techs walked a grid in search of evidence. They also took photographs as potential evidence was discovered. With the body being found on the side of the road, there was a chance that more trash and debris would be dumped as soon as they left. As it stood, it was hard to prevent the cars zooming by from blowing away potential evidence, even with the lane closest to them closed off. There was no guarantee that evidence had not been picked up by the wind and blown away already. Uniformed officers have been ordered to fan out and search, but it was doubtful they would find anything of use.

"There is no way a torture, much less a gruesome murder, took place right next to the interstate and no passing motorists noticed. To perform this kind of torture on someone, the killer needed a private place, somewhere quiet where no one could hear her scream. This was strictly a dumping ground."

"The killer didn't care if the body was found. I'm willing to bet a paycheck this isn't his first kill and he's gotten away with it before. There are no hesitation marks on the body."

"I suspect he isn't going to stop with this one kill either. We need to run the case through VICAP and see if we get similar hits. Let's try to stop him before he kills again."

Sheriff Bradham picked up his phone and called Detective Morris, "I need you and Powell in my office. We need to go over this case and see where we stand. Everyone is afraid this is a serial killer."

"We just pulled up to the department and are on our way in. See you in a minute." Detective Morris knew that Sheriff Bradham would want an update, but there wasn't much to say at this time.

They knocked on the Sheriff's door before entering. He appeared as frazzled as them. "Please tell me you have something. I have the mayor breathing down my neck and concerned citizens calling. The mayor already wants to implement a curfew and call in the FBI."

"Sir, I haven't had a chance to look through VICAP, but that is my next priority. I believe this is the work of a pro. The victim was sexually assaulted, vaginally and anally, before the super glue was applied. She has ligature marks on her wrists and ankles, as well as strangulation marks around her neck. Numerous stab and burn wounds, none contributing to her death, however. All wounds were superficial for the most part. Torture was the prize here and not murder, at least until the very end. She had several cracked ribs and damage to the heart, which the coroner believed was from resuscitation. It looks as if the killer revived her several times before killing her. This would fit with the theory that torture was more important than the actual killing. The coroner also noted that her eyes had been removed.”

“So, this could be the work of a serial killer then. We need to catch this guy before he strikes again.”

The eye removal bothered Detective Morris. He expressed his concerns to his partner, Detective Powell. “This killer is a psycho. Not only did he strangle her and then revive her several times, but he tortured her repeatedly. Did he remove her eyes for a trophy?”

Powell continued to study the photos and autopsy report, “What really bothers me is the precision of the cuts, there seem to be no hesitation marks. The eyes weren’t hacked or gouged out either. They were neatly removed. What did he do with the organs and the eyes? I agree this guy has a screw loose for sure.”

Sheriff Bradham informed the detectives. "Let's get busy then and catch this guy."

A quick search through VICAP for bodies matching the MO of vaginas being super glued resulted in several hits. Some of the bodies found also had Rohypnol in their system. It was something that could be made in your own home with the correct knowledge, or bought on the streets for a price. It was more commonly known as the date rape drug and considered old school now. This could mean they were dealing with someone in their late thirties or early forties, instead of a younger offender. The UNSUB most likely spiked drinks at bars, diners, wherever he found his victims. Once the opportunity presented itself, he moved in and abducted them.

Since he jumped around from state to state, it made it difficult to pin down a pattern and prove that a serial killer was preying on women. After reviewing other case files, they were fairly certain he drove a motor home. A distinct tread pattern had been found at several of the dump sites, all matching a motor home.

The current woman had been sexually assaulted pre and maybe postmortem, bruising around the area was evident. Detective Morris believed the killer was escalating, since the previous victims attributed to the killer were never sexually assaulted. The one common factor was the super glue. Each victim's genitalia had been super glued shut.

This serial killer had definite hunting skills. The killer's MO had changed recently, though. Could it be he had partnered up with someone? The latest victim was skinned and gutted, just like a freshly killed animal. She was cut straight down the middle with great finesse. No hesitation marks were noticed. Why remove the eyes, though? He didn't notice that detail in the VICAP reports.

This killer was meticulous. The cuts were done with almost surgical precision. He had been honing this skill for a while. The coroner suspected that he started skinning and gutting this victim while she was still alive.

Detectives Morris and Powell were currently on their way to follow up with Gabrielle Hurst, the potential victim's roommate, to find out if she could shed any light on Kelly's disappearance and who may have wanted to kill her.

"Kelly sent a text from the bar telling me not to wait up, that she had met a hottie. Supposedly, he was new in town, maybe just passing through. At first, I wasn't worried when she didn't show up the following day, but I knew she had to work on Monday."

"Do you know what bar she frequented or anyone that may have actually wanted to kill her?"

"We had gone bar hopping, but ended up at Harry's on Main Street. That's really the only decent bar to pick up men. We just like to blow off steam and have fun. Neither of us are looking for a permanent relationship. Kelly was a love 'em and leave 'em kind of person. She also had a rough personality. She could be brazen and it got her in trouble quite a bit in the past. Some men didn't like her demeanor at all. It didn't seem to bother her one way or the other. Don't get me wrong now, she was a great person, but you had to know her really well to actually understand her. I think she had a tough childhood and carried a chip on her shoulder. She never talked about her past, though. I think someone hurt her more than she wanted anyone to know."

Morris and Powell made Harry's their next stop. It wasn't 5:00 p.m. yet, but maybe someone was there. A heavy set man with a balding head opened the door. He wore a white t-shirt and jeans, with a bar towel knotted on one of his belt loops. "Sorry fellows, closed for now."

Morris flashed his badge. "Got a couple of questions for you." The smell of stale beer and cigarette smoke annihilated their senses as soon as they walked in the door. Even in the daylight, the bar was dimly lit.

"Now what happened? We haven't had any trouble around here lately officers, so what seems to be the problem?"

"A young lady that frequents the bar was murdered a few nights ago. We are hoping you may remember something or maybe someone else who was here the night she went missing may remember something."

"What night are we talking about?"

"Friday night is supposedly when she was here. She told her friend that she met a new guy in town while here and he was buying her a round."

"Friday night was busy. I don't remember too many faces; they all seem to meld into one after a while. Very few new people venture in here. The bartender will be in at 4:00 p.m., if you want to come back and talk to him. I mainly chitchat with the crowd at the bar just passing time. This is my livelihood and I keep a tight rein around here to keep out the riffraff. I don't want any problems."

"Yes, sir, we understand perfectly. We'll be back later on tonight. Would it be okay to talk to some of the patrons?"

"Sure, most are here by 8:00."

"Thanks a lot."

Morris's phone rang as they walked out of the bar; it was a 703 area code. "Detective Morris."

"Detective Morris, my name is Special Agent Jackson O'Riordan, with the FBI. I understand you have a peculiar murder there."

"Yes, sir, it is a gruesome one, to say the least."

"The hit on VICAP states that there was super glue used on the victim."

"Yes, it was. The woman was also skinned and eviscerated."

"I am tracking down a serial killer with that same signature."

"I believe we may have one of his victims in our morgue then. We just identified the lady today and are retracing her last steps as we speak. She was last seen in a bar not too far from where her body was found. I'm still not sure where she was murdered. Agent O'Riordan there is one new detail you should be aware of, her eyes were also removed. I didn't see that on VICAP."

"No, that is new, but he has been taking small trophies."

***

O'Riordan had a feeling Sheriff Hamilton would receive another package. He needed to call and warn her that this time it would most probably contain the eyes of the latest victim.

O'Riordan decided it would be better to call Alex. With Jordan being pregnant, he didn't want to be the one to break the news to her. "Alex, I thought you would want to know that Jordan will get another package in the mail soon. David may be sending her the victim's eyes."

"I appreciate it, O'Riordan. I'm still trying to figure out where the hell they're going. There is no way they can make it into Canada, not with border patrol the way it is nowadays."

Jordan refused to even look at the package when it arrived in the morning's mail. "Alex, it's here. The task force can have it. I don't even want to open it."

Alex, was intrigued about what the note would say. The note was simple and to the point, "Wish I could see you soon." Alex called O'Riordan to let him know the package from David had been received and sent over to the task force. This time the postmark came from Hampton, Virginia. No one was sure of their destination, but they speculated their next stop might be West Virginia. O'Riordan had already informed the authorities there to be on the lookout. The problem was they were looking for a needle in a haystack.

Chapter 18

Alexandra Jones wasn't sure how long she had been tortured, but she heard her captors talking about disposing of her, after the one named David had his turn.

The will to live was more powerful than the two monsters grueling torture. They both had a hunger for power and control. Each had a need to dominate her and she refused to allow that to happen. She would not show them fear. Her stomach turned from the heady smell of blood in the air. "Stop it!" she told herself. *Those thoughts won't help you out of this mess, now concentrate.* She would outwit them; beat them at their own game, even if every bone in her body did shake in fear.

Alexandra prayed she could actually deceive them and make them believe she was dead. Then, maybe they would just dispose of her body and drive away. All those years of swimming lessons would pay off if this worked. Alex wanted to fake her death before the one named David had his turn. The aura that surrounded him reminded her of pure, incarnate evil. His eyes were empty.

She cringed when the man told his partner, "Hurry up; I'm ready to have a turn with her. Whatever you do, let me finish my fun, before you super glue her best parts closed."

Alexandra didn't know for certain what this guy was talking about, but she knew it wouldn't be pleasant. She had to escape, somehow, someway. When Alexandra felt his hands around her neck, she went into action. She took a deep breath in and held it. She struggled to maintain her control or she would forget to hold her breath. Her heart pounded faster, the sound steadily grew louder in her ears. The jugular vein in her neck began to throb. *Just a little longer, don't give up.* She imagined herself swimming. Her body screamed for air now, but she continued to hold her breath, refusing to give up.

"I'll be damned. I can't believe this bitch is already slipping into unconsciousness."

David asked, "What? What do you mean? I haven't had my turn yet. Slap her, damn it. Let up, you must be squeezing too tight. We can revive her."

"I'm telling you this one is too weak. She is already gone."

Alexandra was thankful, so far they hadn't decided to "revive" her or check for a heartbeat. If they did, then she was doomed. Alex felt someone slapping her face and continued holding her breath. She ignored the pain. She reminded herself that this was her only chance. *Please, please don't let them try CPR. This has to work. I want to live damn it.*

Dumbfounded, The Traveler stated, "Damn. I can't believe this shit. Let's get on the road and dispose of her on the way out of here. We can't stay around here once a body is found anyway. I sure in the hell don't want the smell of a dead body in here. It takes forever to get that smell out."

"Of all the rotten luck. Stupid cunt."

The Traveler didn't even bother wrapping her up. He just discarded her at the camping spot.

Alexandra waited until she heard the vehicle drive away, before she started taking deep breaths. She would wait a while longer before she dared to move. Luckily, they cut her loose from the restraints before disposing of her. They just threw her out like a piece of trash. Alexandra had no idea where she was, but the area reminded her of a campground. Hopefully, there would be other campers around.

The morning sun slowly made its way through the woods and lifted the darkness of the night. Alexandra tried to avoid the road as much as possible, in case her captors were still around. Faint streaks of daylight broke through the heavy woods, creating eerie shadows that seemed to follow her. All around her, she heard the woodland creatures making noise. With each noise, she stopped to make sure it wasn't her captors returning.

The early morning air had a chill to it. Alexandra's breathing became faster with each step. Her eyes were wide open now with terror. The horrific ordeal she just survived remained vivid in her memory. Blood matted in her hair and clung to her face.

Alexandra refused to allow the weariness to stop her feet from moving. Was the nightmare truly behind her? She became terrified that her captors would return. She must find help. She desperately tried to put some distance behind her, venturing deeper into the woods. She didn't want to be found by her captors, not knowing if they had left.

Up ahead, she noticed a building. Could it be an office of some type? Hope entered her mind. Could someone be there? Anyone? Building up her courage, she slowly left her cover of the surrounding woods.

She thought she remembered what their motor home looked like. If only she had gotten a look at the license plate, but she had been too afraid to open her eyes. Not seeing any motor homes nearby, she took a huge chance and walked up to the door. The smell of coffee hit her right away. Her prayers were answered; someone had to be in there brewing coffee. When she tried the doorknob, it turned easily. As soon as she entered the small building, she fell to the floor, exhausted. "Please help me, I've been abducted."

A man rushed to her aid. She felt him gently pick her up, as he talked to her. She was too tired to answer.

Alexandra couldn't stop the flashbacks of the torture she endured while in captivity. At first, her memory was sketchy, to say the least. Then the flashbacks came all at once. They were completely eerie and surreal, as if it was happening to someone else. This couldn't have possibly been done to her. She kept seeing her attackers' faces everywhere. She swore they were watching her, waiting to finish the job. She was terrified to fall asleep, even though the nurses and police officers promised that she was safe.

***

Alex Hamilton couldn't believe it when the FBI called him. A victim had managed to escape. While being tortured, she pretended to be dead. Her captors threw her out of a motor home and took off. She was in rough shape, but alive and able to talk. The FBI wanted him to interview her, since he knew David Thorguson so well. The FBI believed David Thorguson was involved. Maybe after talking to her, he could get into their heads and help capture them before more bodies were found. Even if David Thorguson wasn't involved with this recent abduction, Alex might learn something that would help the FBI locate the woman's captors. Some of the witness's details were fuzzy and maybe he could help clear them up.

Now he had to break the news to Jordan. She wouldn't be too happy, especially since she was due in a few weeks.

"Go Alex. Don't worry about me. Besides, everyone keeps saying your first child is always late. I want these two guys behind bars, if not dead. That way, we know they won't escape again. Hurry up and catch them, so you can come back home."

"I hate leaving you. I can go talk to the witness and come straight back, if you would rather."

"Go, do what you need to do. Catch these two bastards; it's what you do best. Well, one of the things you are good at." Alex saw the twinkle in her eyes, as she made the last comment. He would miss her while he was away. He didn't want to miss the birth of their child, and hoped to wrap this up as quickly as possible.

The FBI had a jet waiting on Alex, just in case he accepted their request. The witness had been brought straight to Quantico, where she was receiving personal medical attention and under heavy guard. The FBI wanted to keep the news of a witness quiet.

Once the plane was in the air, Alex reviewed the notes O'Riordan sent him on the witness. Most of his life had been spent traipsing across the country profiling madmen, working long hours, with no love life. No matter how many of these men Alex helped put away, it seemed like there was another to take his place. At one time, Alex had the ability to disengage himself from the situation, but over the years it became harder to remain unaffected by the horrifying cases he worked. Alex was ready to part ways with the FBI after this case and strike out on his own. He wanted to find out what else life had to offer.

When Alex arrived at Quantico, the gray skies made the day seem even bleaker. On the way to the hospital, Alex felt the rush of excitement when he had a new case to solve. Some of these cases were like puzzles and it required an exorbitant amount of concentration and resolve to solve them. Alexandra was the first woman who saw David Thorguson up close and personal at work and lived to tell about it. She was his first witness that had survived a brutal attack by any serial killer. He was keenly interested in what she had to say. This experience had altered her life forever.

When Alex entered the room, the sight of the witness startled him. She was younger than he expected. Her small body was covered in lacerations, both from the torture and rough terrain of the park. Thankfully, someone was working in the office the morning she escaped.

"Alexandra, my name is Alex Hamilton. I am a former agent helping the FBI find your captors. You're a very brave, young woman. Can I get you anything before I sit down?" Alex tried to put the young woman at ease before he moved in closer. She had been through a very rough ordeal and he didn't want to scare her.

***

Every time Alexandra closed her eyes, she thought she was back in that motor home. She continued to relive the nightmare, even though she had escaped. Or did she escape? She couldn't block the images of the rape, torture, and mutilation out of her mind. The smell of blood still lingered in her nose. Would she ever be a normal human again?

The FBI agent they sent in to talk to her didn't look like any of the other agents. Wait, he did say he was a former agent. That would explain it. He seemed nice enough. Maybe if she told him what all happened to her, he wouldn't judge her. She felt so ashamed.

Alexandra told Alex Hamilton, "The man named David never called the other man by any name. The only one that raped me was David. He had asked the other guy to hold off using the super glue, until he had a chance to have some more fun. I wasn't sure what his plans were with the super glue, but I knew I didn't want to find out. The rape and torture were bad enough." Unfortunately, Alexandra did find out what the super

glue was for. The doctors had informed her that she
would need several surgeries to repair the damage,
and they were not sure if she would ever feel right
down there again. However, Alexandra did not want
another man to touch her ever again. She had never
felt so degraded before.

One of the nurses had suggested a hairstylist be
brought in to fix the young girl's hair. "A good haircut
may help her mood. Every time she looks in the
mirror, she is forced to see all that she had done to
her." Alexandra was surprised at the gesture. She
hated to tell anyone she was afraid to be touched, but
after a while, she did end up relaxing a bit. It was
actually nice to be pampered again.

The hairdresser was taken aback when she arrived.
She was not accustomed to being asked to cut
someone's hair in the hospital. She thought perhaps
this was a cancer patient or someone that needed
uplifting, but when the sedan picked her up and
brought her to Quantico, she didn't know what to
think. Maybe this young girl looking at her was a
soldier, but she was instructed not to ask questions.
"Well, honey, I don't know what the hell happened to
you, but let's see what we can do."

Alexandra was so glad to see a female hairdresser. "I
was in an accident."

"That was a hell of an accident, then."

Alexandra was impressed with the pixie cut; she looked even younger than she was. "Now don't worry my dear, your hair will grow out faster than you think. Whoever did that to your hair should be shot."

Alexandra couldn't help but agree with her. Death was too good for those men. They needed to be put through hell as well

"Now, I think I have some fingernail polish. Why don't we give you an impromptu manicure, while I am here?"

It amazed Alexandra at how a haircut and nail polish had managed to lift her spirits. She thanked Nurse Kelly. "You are so welcome. I'm glad to help you some. I like the haircut. I wish I could wear my hair short, but when it's short, I look just like a boy."

***

Alex was positive this was the work of David Thorguson and the guy who helped him escape. They have a sketch artist coming in to try and get a sketch of the accomplice to post on the news. David Thorguson's mug shot would be used with some variations, in case he had grown a beard or mustache. Sometimes the public had a hard time picturing the face with any type of facial hair. However, David was also a master of disguises. A BOLO had been put out on the motor home.

The manager had a detailed description of the motor home and license plate number, which turned out be to a stolen plate. The driver used a fake driver's license and there was no video surveillance in the office. They never had a problem before that warranted the expense.

The manager of the park was also working with a sketch artist. He only saw one of the men, though. He didn't pick David's photo out of a lineup, so they were hoping he got a good look at the accomplice.

Alex Hamilton needed to talk to O'Riordan. "Agent O'Riordan, I think we may have a break. Alexandra mentioned there was a man called David in the RV. She even managed to pick him out of a photo lineup, except she said that he had a light beard."

If O'Riordan had pushed harder when he first had his suspicions of a potential serial killer, would any of this have happened? "Did she get a good look at the RV they were driving?"

"No. She was too afraid to open her eyes when they dumped her body. She has a vague recollection of it, but that is it."

Agent O'Riordan wished he could get a handle on this case. These two were moving faster than he had expected. "I have a gut feeling that they are building up to something, but what? Where the hell are they going? How many more bodies will be disposed of on the way to their destination?"

Alex was missing Jordan something fierce. She had brought back the joy in his life and kept him from focusing on death. Just the thought of her and their unborn child made him smile. He couldn't wait to get back home. He needed to hear her voice. "How are you doing? Is the baby doing okay?"

"We are doing great, ready for you to get back home."

"It may be a while. The poor girl was abducted and tortured by David Thorguson and his accomplice. He's as messed up as David, and now the torture is getting worse."

"I have complete faith that you will catch them. I miss you and love you very much. Don't worry about us. We aren't going anywhere. I've had the deputies keeping an eye on David's old camp, but there's no sign of life over there. I didn't expect him to come this way; he knew we would be on the lookout for them."

"I worry that he will come after you, but David has no desire to go back to prison. The FBI has no idea how many men or women have been killed. Some bodies were disposed of like yesterday's trash. There is no telling how many bodies are lying in ditches or woods, decomposing."

"David's package came in today. I had the task force come get it."

"They called to say they got it." This package was mild compared to the previous ones. David sent Jordan the poor girl's chopped up hair and a couple of toe nails. The note was another simple note, "She was too weak." If only David knew the irony in that statement.

Agent O'Riordan walked up to Alex as he was finishing his conversation with Jordan. "We are going to go check out the campground, if you're interested."

"Would it be possible to catch a ride with you? I still don't have a rental car. I just jumped on the jet and headed over."

"Let's go. I'm sure we can get you a vehicle afterwards."

"Great. Let's go. Has the local police department checked for evidence?"

"No, they just closed down the campground. Everyone was informed to stay put until they were interviewed and cleared. Only a few people were at the campground. They are waiting on the FBI's forensic techs to get there."

"I doubt our perps are still there. We might get lucky and some trace evidence was left behind."

"I'm hoping someone staying at the campground got a close look at the guy. The park manager is working with the sketch artist now. Maybe we can have a sketch sent out and have identification before we know it."

When Agent O'Riordan and Alex made it to the campground, the forensic techs were finishing up. Agent O'Riordan surveyed the crime scene, trying to imagine it through the killers' eyes. This was a quiet spot, little to no foot traffic. He tried to picture it at night, darkness would envelope you here.

Agent O'Riordan's mood had soured by the end of the day. This deadly duo was pissing him off. He wanted to go back to the hotel bar and knock back a few. David Thorguson and his accomplice seemed to stay one step ahead of them. Where the hell were they going next?

Laughter greeted him as he walked into the bar. He pulled up a stool and waited for the bartender. "What'll it be?"

"*Maker's Mark* and *Sprite*."

"Coming right up."

The first one went down smooth. By the time he had his second, Alex had joined him. "I'll have a Manhattan."

Both drank in silence. A deep frown formed across Alex's face. "I thought this case was over."

"Do you miss profiling?"

"Sometimes, but right now I'm enjoying my life just as it is. I have found a passion in writing and Jordan will be having our first baby soon."

"I'm getting tired of seeing death every day. It can wear you down after a while."

"I hear you."

The next morning, Agent O'Riordan found Alex Hamilton back at the hospital. "Let's go grab a cup of coffee."

In the cafeteria, the smell of hot coffee and bacon welcomed them. "How is she doing?"

Alex thought about it for a moment. "It will be a rough road for her physically and mentally. She was tortured badly, but at least she is alive. David and his partner did a number on her. Now, we need to figure out where they are going next."

"If you are done here, would you be interested in talking to the detectives and other law enforcement personnel working the other cases. Maybe we can figure out where they are headed to or at least come up with a plan of attack."

"Let's go. There's not much more I can do here."

***

Agent O'Riordan was furious when he picked up the morning paper. Dean Albright had somehow managed to find out about Alexandra. Who the hell leaked him the information?

> *A young woman is in critical condition at an unknown hospital after surviving a brutal attack. This young woman is believed to be a victim of a serial killer that has eluded the FBI for years. Sources say she was abducted and somehow managed to escape during the early morning hours. The young woman is working with an FBI sketch artist to help identify her captor(s). Inside sources have revealed the FBI suspects David Thorguson, an escaped convict from Hope, Louisiana, and his accomplice may have been her captors. The FBI, BAU, and ex-profiler Alex Hamilton, have been called in to help with the investigation. Alex Hamilton's experience with serial killers was monumental in the capture of David Thorguson last year. Alex Hamilton has just published his true crime novel on David Thorguson. The book has been on the New York Times bestseller list since its release.*

Alex called O'Riordan as soon as he read the article in the paper. "I hate reporters. How the hell did he find out about her?"

"I wish I knew. Obviously we have a leak somewhere, but who was it? Unfortunately, there are more civilians involved in her escape than we could contain. If it was an FBI agent, there will be hell to pay. At least Dean Albright attached another photo of David Thorguson."

With Dean Albright's recent article and the sketch having gone out to the press, O'Riordan had warned everyone to be ready. There would be many false leads, but they needed to be checked out.

The case took a nosedive after Dean Albright's article ran in the paper. The media went into a frenzy, demanding answers. The story was even picked up by the cable news, causing mass panic in most of the states that David Thorguson and his accomplice had left bodies in. The media made it a point to lay blame on all law enforcement agencies involved. It didn't matter to any of them that the local law enforcement agencies and the FBI were all working hand in hand; blame was being passed around equally.

Chapter 19

The Traveler was ready to get to West Virginia. There was an old family camp nestled on the outskirts of town where they could set up shop. His dad had raised pigs there. He hadn't talked to his family in years, so he didn't know for certain if anyone was living there, but they would soon find out.

Hatred still burned deep in The Traveler's gut. None of those who viciously taunted him deserved to breathe the same air as him. He couldn't wait to exact his revenge and make them pay with their lives. They never considered anyone else's feelings except their own, and now it was his turn to show them there were consequences to playing god. He wanted to see the terror in their eyes as the understanding of what was about to happen to them seeped in. David was right, psychological torture was just as important as physical torture.

First, they needed to pick up some supplies. He would need a generator, wood chipper, and a few other supplies. The Traveler was ready to make the town pay for their cruelty. He'd already divulged his plans to David. David quickly agreed to help punish those who had wronged him.

They arrived in Lake Hamilton, West Virginia forty-eight hours later. Lake Hamilton had always been a small town, with a population well under 35,000. Crime was virtually nonexistent here. Where the surrounding cities had problems with carjacking's, drive by shootings and murder, Lake Hamilton had somehow remained unscathed by these crimes. The worst crime here was an occasional house being burglarized.

Lake Hamilton had always been a vacation spot for the more affluent tourists. A resort was built overlooking the lake years ago. The astronomical green fees for the golf course kept out any unwanted players. The resort and spa had been strategically priced so only the wealthy could afford to vacation here.

Most of the people living in town worked at the resort, spa, or golf course. There were also several restaurants, small businesses, a car dealership, and stores dotted across the town that offered employment to the locals. The coal mines also supported the local economy.

As with any small town, gossip always ran rampant. At least the town wasn't so small that everyone always knew each other's business.

The Traveler knew it was risky coming back here after all this time, but the need for vengeance lured him in. The thrill of retaliation against those that victimized him sent a sizzle of anticipation rushing through his bloodstream. The winds of change were starting to turn. Soon, he would show this town he was the one in control, the one that held their fate in his hands. Revenge would be oh so sweet.

He would make those that were malicious to him pay for all the hurt and indignity they put him through. As time had passed, he hadn't been able to forget about his wretched childhood. Instead, it was all he dwelled on.

The Traveler expressed his concerns to David, "I don't want anyone in town to know I've come back. I want to have the element of surprise on my side. You sure as hell don't need to go anywhere. All we need is for some stupid country bumpkin to recognize you from the news."

"You don't have to worry about me. I plan on keeping a low profile. I have no desire to go back to prison. I'm a master of disguise, though, if and when we do need to venture into town for supplies. We'll be fine, don't worry. We should have enough food to last us a few days. Let's go set up shop and get started. We need to start a list of things we will need for our work room. I didn't get a chance to fully release my hunger with the last one, and I have a need."

For the past year, David had lived in the small, cramped cell, wearing the same thing day in and day out. One year of sleeping on that miserable cot with no privacy whatsoever. One year without anyone to put fear into, torture, have sex with and kill. He never wanted to go back to prison. He would do whatever he had to do to stay free, even if it meant living in squalor.

"Let's go check out our new home, my friend, and get started. Soon, you will be able to satisfy that hunger."

When they arrived at The Traveler's family camp, they discovered it was overgrown. It appeared to have been abandoned for several years. The Traveler couldn't believe it. He hadn't had any contact with his family, so he had no idea if his parents were even alive or if his brother lived here in town. "It doesn't look like anyone has been here for quite some time, so no one will know we are out here. Total isolation. Let's go see how bad it is." The biggest luxury the camp had was running water from a well. David was grateful for this small concession.

David didn't know what to think about the camp. He had assumed this family camp was similar to what he grew up in. This was a shack, literally, and falling apart. One good wind may blow it away. The old barn looked better than where they were supposed to sleep. At least his new friend was correct about the neighbors. David did not see any signs of houses, or life for that matter, on the drive up here. The road to the "camp" was a long, curvy, single lane, gravel road. "This will take some time to get everything right." David warned his friend.

The Traveler didn't see a rundown piece of property; he just saw all the possibilities before them. There may not be much land here, maybe 15 acres, but it was all theirs, to do as they saw fit. The old barn would be perfect for what The Traveler had planned. "Don't worry, my friend. It just needs a little bit of elbow grease. We may find some tools in the barn to use in our workshop. The barn is the best place for us to set up shop. Hell, we may even be able to round up some pigs around here and pin them in. Pigs eat anything and can help with the disposal of the bodies. Let's go see how bad everything really is."

The interior of the barn wasn't in that bad of shape. Mostly cobwebs and a lot of dust. The shack seemed to be sturdy enough. The Traveler even managed to find the old generator for the house.

Proud of the find, he informed David. "It needs a little fine tuning, but we should be able to get the generator running."

David looked at the generator skeptically. "I'm not mechanically inclined at all. I wouldn't know where to start with that."

"Don't worry, my friend. It just takes a little tweaking. I remember this thing from my childhood. My dad would curse this thing to hell and back. Once he was done, he always had it up and running. Here goes nothing." About two hours later, he had indeed kept his word and had the generator running.

"The generator tends to burn a lot of gas. We'll have to keep a steady supply on hand. It may be best not to turn on the thing, unless we need the electricity. During the day, the sun will light up the shack anyway. It's not like we will be catching cable out here."

"I have my own form of entertainment and am itching to get started."

The Traveler couldn't wait to start either. "Well, let's go get our workplace set up."

The Traveler was proud of what they'd accomplished. They transformed the old stalls into mini prisons, with shackles of some type in each one, to keep prisoners from escaping. Hay had been gathered and each stall lined sparsely, but lined nonetheless. Bowls had been placed in each "cage" to help keep their prisoners hydrated. The Traveler would slowly bring his enemies here to be tormented. If they died too soon, he would have to abduct someone else sooner. The psychological torture was just as important as physical torture. The Traveler couldn't wait to get started.

Moonlight streamed in from the windows, mingling with the glow from the lanterns. At the end of the day, both men were weary. Neither had the energy to bother with the generator. Why waste gas when they were going to fall sound asleep? The furnishings were sparse, but David was glad to have a little more breathing room than in the RV. The mattresses smelled musty from the years of abandonment, but at least it was a place to sleep and not a jail cell.

The Traveler felt the eagerness building, churning inside of him. He was one step closer to making his dream a reality. All the years of fantasizing and planning would soon come to fruition. He was ready to unleash his wrath on this town. The anger had been building for so long, and it was time to release it on all those who tormented him before he went insane waiting.

The Traveler noticed David writing a list. "What's up? Do we need more supplies?"

"You know how people always write a bucket list of things they want to do before they die? Well, I'm compiling a list of tortures that have always fascinated me. This little workshop gives me the perfect setting to try a few things, especially with the men." The people they planned on keeping captive here would make the perfect lab rats to perform every sick and twisted fantasy he had ever had.

“That’s a good idea. I can tell you what certain ones were scared of in high school, if you want to use that against them also.”

“This is a team effort, my friend. Remember, psychological torture is just as important as pain.”

Macabre Torture List

Mummification – with a live subject

Length of time it takes for antifreeze to kill the subject

Length of time it takes for rat poison to kill the subject

How long does it take a heart to stop beating after removal from a live subject

Does phantom pain truly exist – removal of a limb from the subject (Must cauterize to keep said subject from bleeding to death)

Does acid being dripped into subject's eye change the eye color?

What happens when the subject ingests lighter fluid and is then forced to swallow hot coals

Is it possible to stretch a subject to death

Confine subject in glass coffin full of spiders

Acupuncture using long hot needles – slowly add burning candles to needles

Bury subject with only head exposed and remove eyelids – let ants and bugs finish off

Make a small incision in gut to pull out the intestines. Restrain subject to tree outside for animals to munch on

Suspend subject above bamboo shoots and wait for them to grow into the subject.

Chapter 20

Dylan Robinson took over the car dealership after his dad had his heart attack. He had been waiting for years to say the dealership was officially his. Being a Robinson in this town meant something. They were looked up to. He craved power. Even in school it gave him a superiority complex. In any other town Dylan would be a peon, here he was a member of the elite.

The Traveler watched as Dylan walked to his Lexus. Of course, Dylan couldn't drive a car from his family's dealership. Whatever vehicle he drove must have snob appeal, a show of money. Even the way Dylan dressed screamed money, from his Armani double-breasted suit, and crisp white shirt with his red silk tie.

Dylan would be the first one in line for retribution. For years Dylan tormented The Traveler. Now it was his turn. Dylan would experience pain like he had never imagined.

The Traveler was pleased with the disguise David came up with for him. Unless he told you who he was, you would never know.

The Traveler walked up to Dylan's car and knocked on the window. "Dylan, long time old buddy."

Dylan couldn't place the face, but if there was a chance this guy wanted to buy a car, he would play along. "How have you been?"

"You don't recognize me, do you?"

Dylan didn't recognize the man at all. "I'm sorry, but I'm having a hard time putting a name to the face."

The Traveler gave him a sinister leer. "That's okay. I came back in town to settle some old debts. You're the first."

Dylan felt a shock run through his body. That was the last thing he remembered.

***

Dylan heard a voice talking to him, waking him up. The person sounded far off. The Traveler heard Dylan moaning, but he still hadn't woken up. He couldn't wait any longer, he was ready for Dylan to wake up and face his demons. The Traveler grabbed a bucket of water and dumped it over Dylan's head.

Dylan was awake now. He was cursing up a storm, muttering all kinds of profanities. A hint of alarm reached his voice when he realized he was immobile.

"I need you awake, so I can show you who is in control. I have a buddy who wants to help me, but I have to warn you he's been compiling a list of various torture techniques. They are indeed quite intriguing. He is feeling rather impatient right now, as he has been unable to experiment with his tortures in a while. I'm afraid that he may not be able to control himself."

David looked over at The Traveler, "I haven't decided which torture our first victim should undergo. There are so many to choose from."

"Well, my friend, I say this one needs to be buried, so the ants can play with him. He always had a way about him with the ladies; maybe the ants will find him just as sweet."

"I like the way you think."

"It's a quirk of mine, but I must super glue his penis closed. I've been told the pain is excruciating."

Dylan was still secured to the chair, for the time being. His wrists were bloody from where the straps had cut into him. He had desperately been trying to escape, but the restraints refused to budge.

"So, Dylan, you remember all those years of hell you put me through? Now it's my turn. I seem to remember you telling me God should never have given me a pecker, because I would never use it. Well, now you won't use yours ever again." Pure venom dripped from The Traveler's words. Hatred seeped from his very pores. The veins in The Traveler's neck bulged with every word he spoke. "It's time for reckoning, Dylan."

When Dylan looked into his captor's eyes, he realized who this man was. With sickening clarity, he knew he was doomed. There was no way this man would let him escape. He would finally pay for the sins of his past. His only hope was reasoning with the man, but from the look in his eyes that may not be possible. "We were kids back then. It was harmless fun."

"Well then, I plan on having some harmless fun with you too; my fun may be a little more painful."

Dylan always thought he had a high tolerance for pain, but the pain associated with the super glue going into his penis had to be the worst he had ever felt. He couldn't stop the tears that flowed down his cheeks.

"Aww, what's wrong, Dylan? Not man enough for the pain? What kind of man are you? My friend here grew up in your social circle, but he treats me with respect. We are kindred spirits.

"I should warn you, though. He is an escaped convict. He killed over nineteen women, before the police captured him. Don't worry, though; I'm not ready to kill you just yet. I want you to endure the torment for as long as I can keep you alive. Your friends will be joining you shortly."

Dylan hated this feeling of complete powerlessness. He's always been the one in control.

***

It would take some time to dig the hole, and The Traveler still wanted to have some fun with him before burying him. After he applied the super glue, he pulled out a knife. He made slow, steady cuts on Dylan's chest, making sure each one was more consistent with a nick than anything deeper. After each cut, The Traveler rubbed salt into the wound. He watched Dylan's eyes dilate with fear, then pain with each cut. After a while, Dylan was squirming and writhing in agony. His eyes were dull and glassy. It would do him no good to have Dylan die too early. Where would the entertainment be in that, after all?

Once David finished digging the hole, he felt his control slipping. He had watched his friend torture the man slowly and deliberately. "Come on, my friend, I need to quench this hunger I have."

"I don't want you to lose control, just yet. I want to keep him alive a bit longer. Once he has served his purpose, we can dispose of his body here. I managed to capture two hogs today and one is a big mean sow. In a few days, they will be good and hungry."

David knew he couldn't kill the man, but he still felt a need to implement some kind of pain on him. He needed the rush desperately, he was having major withdrawals. Picking up a hammer from one of the workbenches, he strolled over to Dylan. After checking the straps, he picked up the hammer and took aim for one of Dylan's feet. With a mighty swing, the hammer made contact with Dylan's foot. In that instant, you heard bones crunching. The man's screams were music to his ears. He repeated the process on the other foot and then his hands. By the time David was done, he had managed to break both of Dylan's hands and feet. When Dylan passed out from the pain, they transferred him to the hole and buried him neck deep. They would wait for him to wake up again before removing his eyelids. That pleasure would go to The Traveler.

Even after being tortured, Dylan had a pompous arrogance about him. After hours of torture, Dylan still didn't understand that money wouldn't save him. The Traveler would break him.

***

Intense pain pulled Dylan out of unconsciousness. He felt as if his face was on fire, and for some reason, he couldn't move from the neck down. He looked down and realized he was buried from the neck down in a hole. He remembered now where he was. He began to panic when he realized the crawling sensation on his face must be the ants as they bit into his tender flesh. He tried to blow a puff of air through his nose to expel the ants that were in there. They were crawling all over his eyes and in his ears. He tilted his head one way, then the next to extract them from his ears. He couldn't scream or they would crawl into his mouth.

His eyes darted around to see a long, steady line heading his way.

***

David was thrilled with the prospect of starting on his list of macabre tortures. He planned to start a journal of sorts to keep track of his successes.

To help with disposal of the bodies, they had previously set up the wood chipper The Traveler discovered in the shed. This would allow them to dispose of the body straight into the pig pens. The pigs should devour the remains, as if they were a delicacy. Now, David was finally free to work without any limitations.

***

Josh Thompson wondered where his oldest brother was. It wasn't like Dylan to be late. Dylan had to be the greediest person he knew. That man dreamed of money.

Josh tried Dylan's cell phone, but the call went straight to voicemail. His car was here, but he was nowhere around. Josh was starting to worry. His brother never missed a call. Hell, he probably answered the phone while banging some chick.

There was no answer at Dylan's house either. Where the hell could that man be?

Josh called his parents' house. "Mom, is Dylan over there by any chance?"

"No, hun, I haven't seen him."

Where the hell was he then? "If you see him, please have him call me."

"You know Dylan; he's probably at the dealership."

"Yes ma'am. I'm heading there now." There was no sense worrying her right now.

Josh decided to open up and wait. It wasn't like he couldn't run the business.

By lunchtime, no one had seen or heard from Dylan. Dylan still wasn't answering his cell phone either. Josh decided it was time to go ask Sheriff Ourso for help. The Sheriff's Office wasn't far from the dealership, so Josh decided to walk over there. On the way back, he could pick up some lunch. It was too nice of a day to drive, and the exercise would do him some good. Unlike his brother Dylan, Josh always had a hard time with his weight and he wanted to lose a few extra pounds.

Josh noticed the receptionist at the Sheriff's Office and his palms became sweaty. He had had a crush on Nancy Jarvis since high school, but she probably didn't even know he existed. "Good afternoon, Nancy. Is Sheriff Ourso in?"

"Hi Josh, how have you been doing? Sheriff Ourso is in his office. I'll let him know you are here."

"Thank you so much, and I'm fine by the way. So, how are things going for you?" Josh couldn't believe he was having a conversation with her. He bumbled through his words just to keep the conversation going.

"It's good. I'm so ready for lunch, though. Today is dragging by. It's been really quiet, which is good, I guess."

Josh gathered up his nerve and asked, "Well, if you are interested, after I speak with Sheriff Ourso, I can take you out to lunch."

Nancy felt her pulse quicken a little; she couldn't believe that Josh Robinson had just asked her out. "I would love that."

Nancy called back to Sheriff Ourso's office. "Sir, Josh Robinson is here to see you."

Sheriff Ourso wondered what in the world Josh Robinson would need to see him for. "Send him on back."

"Afternoon, Mr. Robinson, what brings you over here?"

"Sheriff, have you seen Dylan? I can't find him anywhere. I've tried his cell and home phone, but he isn't answering either. I'm worried. This isn't like him. You and I both know his world revolves around work."

Sheriff Ourso knew Josh meant to say money, but let it drop. "I haven't seen him. I can send out a patrol car to his house. Have you tried his girlfriend? Maybe he stayed there last night."

"Dylan doesn't have a regular girlfriend. He didn't mention anything about a date last night."

"We'll check things out and let you know. Maybe he is finally taking a break and enjoying life."

Chapter 21

The Traveler never liked preying on victims during the day, but with David's expertise in disguises, they were able to run into town. They also needed a few supplies and were low on gas. While at the hardware store, they also purchased some drain cleaner. David's new friend had a trick on debilitating a potential victim. Plus, The Traveler wanted to get back at Heather for leaving burning bags of shit on his porch.

"We put a pouch of drain cleaner in a plastic bottle with just a small amount of water. When the person picks it up, it creates a small explosion. I don't use enough Drano to hurt them, but enough to disorient them so that I can move in. I already have my next prisoner picked out. I believe you will enjoy this next one, it is a female." The Traveler knew David was getting sexually frustrated. He could take out his frustrations on Heather.

They sat outside of Heather Vaughn's house and watched as she opened her front door and walked out onto her porch. She saw the old bottle of soda next to the paper and grabbed it from the bottom. Before Heather fully understood what was happening, a small explosion occurred.

The Traveler moved in quickly and knocked her out with chloroform before she could wake up the whole neighborhood with her screaming. "This was a lot better than all those burning bags of dog shit you would leave on my front porch, don't you think? You should have been nicer to me."

Heather didn't hear a word he said. She was already out.

***

Heather slowly woke up. She felt as if she had been hit by an 18-wheeler. Her eyes burned like crazy and she was having a difficult time seeing anything. Everything was one big blur. Her arms were restrained to the wall. The air was cool and damp against her skin. What was happening? Why was she shackled and naked?

She desperately pulled at the restraints. She felt a ray of hope grow in her heart when the screws holding the shackles to the wall gave some. Maybe if she just pulled a little harder.

She heard footsteps and someone talking. Her heart sank.

"Heather, do you remember in elementary school when you and your friends used to pick on me, always calling me short. Maybe the real reason was that you were just self-conscious and always wanted to be taller. I'm going to give you the chance to actually be taller, and slimmer."

"Let's get her on the rack and start off by stretching her body. While she is being stretched, I can toy with her." It had been a while since David had had sex and he was about to burst with need.

"You were a very, bad girl and need to be punished." She tried to block out his voice. A tiny whimper escaped her. She despised showing him any kind of weakness.

Heather felt the pain coming at her from all directions. Besides being slowly stretched, each man was torturing her in some way. While one man raped her with so much force that she feared she would split in half, the other man entertained himself by choking or cutting her.

The pain dulled her mind. She could hardly think clearly at all now. Her tormentor stared down at her with such a menacing glare. Hate seemed to exude from him.

***

The pain and indignation from his childhood boiled over inside him. David was teaching him how to channel that pent up rage into the torture of the victims. The Traveler decided to let the rage guide him. He tuned out the screams as David repeatedly raped her. Hell, it didn't even bother him that David had joined in and they were both torturing her at the same time.

The Traveler finally felt superior to those in this town. Now, who should their next victim be?

David pulled out his journal to update today's entries.

Chapter 22

The neighborhood was an upper class development, built alongside Lake Hamilton. Each lot was at a minimum two acres, but most average five acres. The houses, or mini mansions, were made up of stucco and imported lumber with well-manicured lawns. There was more than enough living space for any of the families living here. The development was a gated community with its own private golf course and a clubhouse, which offered tennis courts, a heated pool, and a hot tub. Nothing was too good for the people who lived here. The starting price for houses here was over one million dollars.

 Why did they have to be so greedy? Everything around here seemed to revolve around money and who had it. You were considered a "nobody" if you didn't have money, but that was about to change. He would show them who was in control of their future.

Michael and Jill Redmond enjoyed throwing lavish parties at their house. Dylan Thompson and Heather Vaughn didn't show up tonight and everyone speculated about where they were. Dylan hadn't been seen in almost a month. His family was extremely worried. Supposedly, no word had been heard from either of them. Heather was probably somewhere enjoying her new found freedom, spending her ex-husband's money to spite him. If it hadn't been for her not showing up tonight, Jill wondered if anyone would have even noticed Heather missing. Lately, Heather seemed to alienate everyone from her life.

The Traveler and David were able to get into the neighborhood easily, due to the Redmonds' party. They just informed the security guard that they were with the caterer. Darkness shrouded the back of the house.The houses were far enough apart that they didn't have to worry about being seen by a neighbor. The men watched until everyone had left.

David looked over at his friend, "Let's go around back and surprise them. We just want to knock them out for now. Make sure the lights are all out, before pulling the car out of the garage."

It was a risky move, driving around in the couple's Mercedes, but someone would surely notice a bundle in the back of the truck.

"We can also ransack the house for any food."

David agreed. "We just want to be quick, in and out as fast as possible."

They saw Michael stepping outside to put out the trash and attacked him, dragging his unconscious body inside. David went after the wife, while The Traveler searched for the car keys. They loaded the couple and items in the SUV. David would drive their vehicle back, while his friend drove the truck back to the hideout.

Both were anxious to get started. David enjoyed the psychological torture that was involved in a double killing and the anticipation was too much.

The Traveler always hated growing up in poverty, but at this very minute, he was thankful for it. He was able to teach David how to live off of the land. Rabbits were plentiful around the old camp, so they didn't have to worry about starving to death. As winter moved in, they may have to rethink their hideout. Pilfering through their victims' houses had helped stock their pantry with food items and they also managed to find quite a few useful items for their workshop, not to mention stocking up on gas cans and gas. Murder was paying off.

Macabre Torture Journal

Length of time it takes for antifreeze to kill subject – Test subject Michael has had small amounts of antifreeze added to his water. His psychological torture included watching his wife endure being raped repeatedly and various tortures implemented on her body.

Is it possible to stretch a subject to death? Test subject Heather has been stretched more. Some discomfort noticed. She still attempts to writhe away while being raped. Some fight remains in her.

As he finished writing in his journal, David thought about his sweet Detective. Correction, she was sheriff now, even better. He wanted to finish what he'd fantasized about with her. He wanted to watch the blood ooze from her body. The bitch, she enjoyed locking him up. This current victim would have to satisfy the fantasies he had about his sweet Sheriff, for now. David wondered if his sweet sheriff knew he was thinking of her at this moment.

***

Sheriff Hamilton felt goose bumps crawl up her spine. It was as if someone had walked over her grave.

Chapter 23

Sheriff Ourso had just arrived at the office Monday morning, when he saw Michael Redmond, Sr. pull up. Sheriff Ourso assumed something big must be going on for Michael Sr. to be away from his law office. That man constantly thought about work.

"Sheriff, I haven't heard from Michael and Jill all weekend. They had a big party Saturday night at their house, but Michael did not show up at work today. I figured when they didn't show up for church on Sunday, they were just recouping from Saturday night, but Michael knew we had a lot of meetings set up for today. They aren't answering any of their phones and I didn't see them at their house. Michael's Mercedes ML430 SUV is gone, but Jill's BMW 750Li is in the garage."

Sheriff Ourso didn't like this one bit. No one had heard from or seen Dylan Robinson and now another prominent couple from here may be missing. "Mr. Redmond, let's go check out their house and see if you notice anything missing."

Sheriff Ourso pulled up to the guard shack, "Sheriff Frank Ourso to see Michael and Jill Redmond."

"Yes, sir." Sheriff Ourso maneuvered his car through the gates. The Redmonds' house was the largest one in the gated community. Sheriff Ourso wondered what they needed with all this space. Not only was the house massive, but there was a four-car garage attached to the house with a second story. The landscaping was impeccable. Someone had put a lot of effort into the care and nurturing of the grounds.

Before going into the Redmonds' house, Sheriff Ourso gave further instructions, "Mr. Redmond, if you'll unlock the door, I'll go in first and check things out. Once it is clear, I'll have you walk around with me to see if anything is missing."

"Yes, sir, but I went in there earlier and didn't see anyone here."

"I just want to make sure everything is safe, sir."

Sheriff Ourso came back a few minutes later to get Mr. Redmond. "Okay, sir; let's go see if you notice anything missing."

They started in the kitchen. "I know they just had a big party, but it was catered. There is no food at all in the house, even the pantry is empty. That's out of character for Jill. Even though she very seldom cooks, she likes having a few staples on hand for impromptu gatherings."

Mr. Redmond walked into Michael's home office, "It looks as if the safe wasn't touched. I'm not sure how much money Michael keeps on hand, but money and Jill's jewelry are still in here. It's hard to say, but I don't think the house was robbed. I'm not sure what the deal with the food missing is, but where the hell are Michael and Jill. Both of their cell phones are still on the charger. Jill doesn't go anywhere without her phone or purse, and both are still here."

They walked out back to Michael's workshop. "It's hard to say, but I don't see any gas cans and it appears that someone has been rifling through the tools and things. I wouldn't know for sure if anything was missing here, though."

Sheriff Ourso had a bad feeling about this. "Mr. Redmond, I'm going to send a crime scene crew over here to dust for fingerprints. I don't like this one bit."

Sheriff Ourso wasn't sure what was going on, but they had three people that he knew of, who seemed to have vanished into thin air. "Mr. Redmond do you know who all was at the party Saturday night? I need to talk to them. Maybe they noticed something out of place."

"I know Heather Vaughn, Maria Henderson, Barbara Swanson, Randy Jenkins, and Stephen and Adele Fisher were all invited. I'm sure they invited more people, but I'm not sure who else. Those two love to entertain, and it's usually the same group of friends that come over. Most of them have been friends since they were in grade school."

"Thank you. I'll go and talk to them. We'll get this all worked out."

No one answered at Heather Vaughn's house. Maybe Sheriff Ourso could catch Maria at her office. He asked the receptionist, "Is Ms. Henderson in this morning?"

"She sure is, Sheriff Ourso; I'll let her know you are here."

Maria Henderson greeted him at the front desk. "Good morning, Sheriff. What can I do for you?"

"Did you happen to attend the party at Michael and Jill Redmond's house on Saturday night?"

"Yes, sir, I sure did, as well as a few of our other friends. Let's go back to my office, so we can sit and talk."

She led him back to her office. "I didn't think to ask you if you would like anything to drink."

"I'm fine. Michael and Jill Redmond seem to have disappeared. I wanted to see if you noticed anything unusual?"

"Everything had been the same as always. We ate, drank, and talked. The only people that didn't come were Dylan Robinson and Heather Vaughn. We talked about how Dylan's family was worried about him. We all figured Heather was on a beach somewhere spending her ex-husband's money just to piss him off."

"So Heather Vaughn wasn't there either?"

"No, she wasn't. Come to think of it, I don't remember the last time I talked to Heather. Like I said, we figured she was off enjoying her new found freedom. Her ex-husband is a major asshole. He wasn't from around here and he moved back to wherever he was from."

Sheriff Ourso worried if Heather Vaughn was missing or out partying. He'd have to go by Heather's house and check things out there too.

After knocking on her door and not getting an answer, he looked into the garage. Her car was still there. He wondered why she wasn't answering her door. There was also a pile of newspapers at the end of the driveway.

"Sheriff, I haven't seen Heather in a while." The sheriff turned around to see one of Heather's neighbors, Pam Harrison, in the yard.

"Do you know if she had planned a trip?"

"She didn't say anything. If she plans to be gone for a few days, she usually asks me to get her papers for her. She doesn't want everyone to know she is gone. She is always paranoid that someone will let her ex-husband know. She moved in right after her divorce was final. From what I understand, she sold her other house cheap just to piss off her ex. She really enjoys aggravating him when she can, even if he isn't living here in town anymore."

Sheriff Ourso knew without a missing person's report or extenuating evidence, he couldn't go bursting inside. "If you happen to see Ms. Vaughn, would you please ask her to give me a call?" Sheriff Ourso slid a note under her door, just in case she was sleeping.

He wondered what the hell was going on around here. It wasn't like some of these people to just get up and leave.

Chapter 24

When they ran into a neighboring town for gas, David couldn't resist the urge to send Sheriff Jordan Hamilton some flowers. He noticed a coffee shop with Internet, which was perfect for his needs. The gas station had prepaid VISA's for sale, which would help keep anyone from tracing his steps.

"I will be right back. I have something to do."

The Traveler had learned not to ask David too many questions. The man could be close-mouthed at times. "Let's meet at the local hardware store."

David went to the FTD website and ordered a small bouquet. He wanted to let her know he was thinking of her. The card read, "Miss me yet".

David knew there was no way to trace where the flowers came from and tracing the VISA was useless. He wished he could see the look on her face when she received the flowers. Was Mr. FBI around to comfort her or was he trying to track them down. Good luck with that. They were states away from Louisiana.

As David walked down the aisles of the hardware store, he found one of his favorite chemicals to use on victims, muriatic acid. He wanted to add this to his arsenal. If only he had access to his money. He wasn't used to watching what he spent. However, he was getting quite good at the five finger discount. Unfortunately, the container of acid was too big to hide on him. At least it wasn't that expensive.

* * *

Jordan was excited when she walked up to her door and saw the flowers. She couldn't believe Alex took time out of his busy schedule to send them to her. Since she wasn't sure exactly how busy he was, she decided to send him a quick text. "Of course I miss you. Both baby and I are thinking about you right now." She included a picture of the flowers, so he could see what the florist sent.

A few seconds later, her phone rang. "I hope I didn't disturb you with the text, but I wanted to thank you for the flowers."

"Honey, exactly what did the card say?"

"Stop being silly, it said that you miss me, of course."

"Jordan, as much as I would love to take the credit for the flowers, I didn't send them."

Jordan went pale and had to sit down. "Damn that man. Why does he have to be the one who is constantly sending me flowers? I'm really beginning to hate the idea of flowers being delivered now."

"I'm so sorry, Jordan. Can you tell what florist they came from?"

"They were delivered in an FTD box and left by the door."

"You know the drill, don't touch anything. I'm going to call the FBI office in Springport and have them send an agent to get everything. I'm also going to request they put a detail on you, until this guy is caught."

"Alex, don't be ridiculous. I can take care of myself. Besides, they are probably miles from here."

"Humor me. You aren't able to maneuver around as easily as you were the last time David Thorguson had you in his sights. I'd feel a lot better knowing someone is watching over you, until he is behind bars."

"Good save. It looks like I swallowed a bowling ball right now. I'll humor you this one time, but I don't think he's anywhere around here."

"Neither do I, but I would rather be safe than sorry. I don't want anything to happen to either of you. I love you both very much."

"We love you too. Be safe."

Chapter 25

As Sheriff Ourso was leaving for the night, Mr. Robinson came into the office. He felt bad for Mr. Robinson; he stopped by almost every night to see if there had been any new development on Dylan and the other missing persons.

"Sheriff Ourso, have you found my son yet?"

"No, sir, I'm sorry we haven't found him or the others yet. We are trying our best to locate them. We just have not had any breaks in the case as of yet."

"What else can I do to help?"

"Sir, you have done everything you can. Dylan's photo has been posted all over town and the story has even been picked up by the news networks. The paper runs an article at least once a week about the missing people in town. We just aren't getting any good leads."

"He's out there somewhere. You must find him! Have you searched the lake, just in case they are dead?"

"Yes, sir, we had some divers volunteer their time and equipment to search the area and they didn't find anything."

"How long ago was that? I'll pay them to search again."

"Mr. Robinson, they aren't there. As soon as I hear something, you will be the first to know. Do you want me to drive you home?"

Tears formed in Mr. Robinson's eyes. "No, I'm going to go over to the dealership and check on Josh."

Sheriff Ourso knew Mr. Robinson was overcome with grief and was frustrated that his son hadn't been found. If only there was something more that he could do.

It was well after dark when Sheriff Ourso made it home. He walked inside and let the darkness envelop him. His heart and mind were heavy and he was just so damn tired. They were no closer today than they were in the beginning to finding the missing persons.

He slowly made it into the main part of the house and turned on some lights. He wasn't hungry, but he should eat something. He looked out into the night and wondered where they were. The missing people had to be alive, somewhere out there. He wanted nothing more than to find them and bring their families some relief from the overwhelming grief they must be feeling right now.

He poured a scotch and water before worrying with supper. He was digging through the fridge for leftovers when he heard a knock at the door. It was Hannah.

Frank was glad to see her. "This is a pleasant surprise."

"I missed seeing your face and figured you may want supper. I fixed shrimp scampi and a cheesecake for dessert."

"Sounds perfect. I was digging through the refrigerator, looking at the leftovers."

After supper, they settled down on the couch to watch television. Hannah tilted her head up and pressed her lips to his. He returned the kiss with an increasing fervor.

Kissing Hannah, Frank let his thoughts drift away, focusing on her and the way she made him feel. He threaded his fingers through her hair and kissed her deeper, bringing her closer to him. He let his hands wander over her body, marveling at her feel. He stroked her back, kneading her muscles. He felt her slowly unbutton his shirt, pushing it off of him. He lightly massaged her breasts, teasing her nipples. Heat radiated from her body.

Frank picked her up and carried her to the bedroom. He placed her on the bed and removed her clothes. His mouth found her bare breast and suckled gently. Hannah let out a moan, as desire overcame her. "I need you now."

She rolled on top of him and took him into her mouth, teasing him, as he teased her. His breathing became labored. "Hannah, I want to be inside you, now. You are driving me crazy." His thrusts became faster and

more urgent, until they both climaxed together.
Panting heavily, they both screamed out together,
coming hard.

Chapter 26

Blood splatter stained the wood in their workshop. David preferred to have a clean area when he worked. "We need to get some bleach the next time we go into town. Let's clean this place up a little bit. I'm not too keen on all the blood splatter; it's starting to draw flies."

"Maybe our next victim will have a pressure washer in their shed."

"Good thinking."

Moonlight streamed in from the open windows and doors of the workshop. Her skin was already slick from sweat mixed with blood, causing it to gleam in the moonlight's glow. David took a deep breath, forcing his body to relax. Their next victim reminded him of his sweet sheriff back in Hope, Louisiana. He was trying to keep his self-control in check. He didn't want to rush things; slow and steady.

He could see their newest victim trembling. Good, she is already scared.

The victim's blood slowed to a drip, rather than a steady flow. The Traveler and David had installed the shackles to the rafters earlier in the day. They even located some bamboo to plant underneath her. David didn't want it growing too fast. When he read about this ancient torture technique on the internet, it enthralled him.

They had also installed meat hooks into the rafters. The meat hooks would allow them to contort the body in different positions. The workshop was now transformed into something they could be proud of.

Outside, the pigs smelled the blood in the air and began to cause a ruckus. Over the last few days, David and he had managed to trap five more, giving them a total of seven. The pigs were getting nice and hungry; the bodies should be devoured in record time, if one did finally pass away. Currently, they were all still being tortured.

The body hanging from their latest contraption was Maria Henderson, a forty year old real estate agent. One day, during their sophomore year, he had asked Maria out on a date. She had the audacity to spit in his face and laugh at him. She informed him that there was no way she would be caught dead with a country hick like him. Well, he would get the last laugh on this one. Of course, it would be fun torturing her for a while before killing her. David seemed to like her too, and The Traveler was sure he would have a lot of degrading sex acts to perform on her.

Life was looking up for The Traveler. People were slowly disappearing around town and no one had a clue as to their whereabouts.

For a single lady, Maria Henderson had a variety of useful tools and gadgets in her garage. They hit the jackpot there. She did indeed have a pressure washer, plus another generator and two freezers stocked full of food. Inside the house, they found more food, bleach, and other cleaning products. By the time they finished loading the truck and Maria's car, there was barely any room left for her.

The truck had been a lucky find. An elderly lady had wanted to get rid of her late husband's truck for next to nothing. With all the cash they had managed to steal from the latest victims, purchasing the truck wasn't a problem. It also helped them stay inconspicuous around town. Eventually, someone would have recognized the motor home coming into town at least once a month.

David pulled out his journal to update today's entries.

Macabre Torture Journal

Length of time it takes for antifreeze to kill subject – Test subject Michael has had small amounts of antifreeze added to his water. Forced him to watch, as wife was raped and sodomized.

Is it possible to stretch a subject to death? Test subject Heather has been stretched more. Several joints appear to be dislocated.

Acupuncture using long hot needles – slowly add burning candles to needles. Test subject Jill now has three needles inserted and rotating the sites of burning candles.

Bury subject where only head was exposed and remove eyelids – let ants and bugs finish off. The test subject did not respond to continued torture.

Suspend subject above bamboo shoots and wait for them to grow into test subject. Test subject Maria has been chosen for this torture. Currently waiting for bamboo to grow. As a bonus, test subject did not like being raped and cried during the process.

***

Caylee Habersham had worked as the receptionist for Maria Henderson for five years now. Maria had never missed a day of work and now it had been two days since Caylee heard from her. Caylee knew Maria had been worried about several of her friends going missing, and now Caylee was worried about Maria. She walked over to the Sheriff's Office to see if he was in.

"Is Sheriff Ourso in today?"

"He is in his office. Let me get him for you."

It didn't take long for Sheriff Ourso to come up front. "What seems to be the problem, Caylee?"

"Sheriff, Maria Henderson hasn't shown up for work for two days now. I wasn't worried when she didn't show up yesterday, but she missed a house showing this morning and that's not like her. If she doesn't sell a house, we don't get paid."

"Do you have the address of the house she was supposed to show?"

"Yes, sir, I made you a list of where all she had talked about going yesterday and today. Yesterday, she had planned to check on some investment properties for a few clients and today she had showings."

"Thanks, I'll get right on this."

After checking her house, Sheriff Ourso had a bad feeling in the pit of his stomach. Just like at the Redmonds' house, Maria's house had been wiped clean of all food. It also appeared that someone went through her shed and garage, but he wasn't sure if anything was missing.

As of yet, no one had heard from Heather Vaughn either. He needed to obtain a search warrant and check out the interior of Heather's house.

After opening the front door, the mustiness from the house being closed up hit Sheriff Ourso. There was a lamp on in the living room and the house wasn't immaculate, but clean. It had a lived in look. The living room was quite large for the size of the house and filled with expensive furniture. There wasn't an empty space left in the room.

Sheriff Ourso moved on to the kitchen. There were dishes in the kitchen sink, and from the look of it, they had been there a while, since mold was starting to grow on them. He could add Heather's name to the growing list of missing.

Chapter 27

Barbara Swanson couldn't wait to hit the hiking trails this morning. The morning sun was starting to peek over the horizon. The sky came alive with soft hues of pink and orange. The dew glistened on the grass, shimmering like tiny diamonds when the sunlight hit it. Barbara loved to watch the sunrise in the park. It gave the place such a magical quality. She breathed in the morning air, smelling the damp earth. She had everything ready to go. Randy Jenkins planned to meet her near the park office at 6:00 a.m. It would be a picture-perfect day.

Randy and Barbara had dated during high school, then went their separate ways during college. Now that they were both recently divorced, they were taking up where they left off in high school. So far, things were going dreamily.

Barbara could already feel the stress leaving her body from the hectic work week as soon as she pulled into the park's parking lot. She couldn't wait to hit the hiking trail. She wondered where Randy was. The only vehicle in the lot right now was a motor home. She started to remove her hiking equipment out of her car while she waited for him to arrive. A few minutes later, she heard Randy drive up.

Daybreak was fast approaching. Sunlight was starting to filter through the trees. A shadow fell across them as they geared up. Barbara heard someone calling Randy's name.

The Traveler called out to Randy. "Randy, Randy Jenkins? Is that really you?"

Randy looked up to see who was calling him. Randy felt a jolt of electricity go through him. He noticed Barbara going down. What the hell was going on?

***

The Traveler heard Randy talking about his hiking trip while shopping at the hardware store. Instead of going back to the hideout, they drove to the park to wait. The Traveler doubted too many people would be out this early on a Saturday morning.

The Traveler wished he could go back in time and relive his teenage years. Instead of cowering like a little girl from those that bullied him, he would fight back. Growing up, no one would stand up to those in the "elite group". Those damn namby pamby kids always thought they were better than the rest of the town. He would show them who was in control now.

The Traveler took pride in his good looks. After all, they didn't come to him easily. During his teenage years he was a tall, lanky kid that shied away from everyone and everything. Now, he was a muscular man and some women told him he reminded them of a movie star.

Those that he had abducted here in town had to do a double take to recognize him. The Traveler enjoyed showing the jackals of this town he had control over their lives now. Anger and hatred festered deep in his gut.

***

The park ranger noticed the two cars still in the parking lot the next morning. Neither car looked like they had moved overnight. Where could the owners be? He decided it would be best to call the sheriff and let him know, just in case they had an injured couple along one of the trails. He also needed to call in several other park rangers so that a thorough search could be conducted.

"Sheriff, this is John Meyers over at the park. I just wanted to let you know we have a couple of cars that have been in the lot over twenty-four hours. I am arranging a search right now, but if you have any spare men, we would appreciate the help."

"If you can give me the license plate numbers, I'll run them for you and give you their names."

"No need, I know who the vehicles belong to. Randy told me about a hiking trip he had planned. He wanted to know which trail to take for a little seclusion. The vehicles belong to Randy Jenkins and Barbara Swanson. I've checked both restrooms and neither are there. I've also called Randy's cell phone, but it goes straight to voicemail. Randy isn't answering his house phone either."

"I'll send a deputy to each of their houses and let you know if they are there. I'll also round up some volunteers to help with the search. Are you sure they headed out on the trail you recommended?"

"I can't guarantee it. Barbara is an avid hiker around here, so she may have suggested another trail."

Sheriff Ourso arranged for search and rescue to meet up with him at the park in half an hour. The dispatcher was calling the remaining deputies back on duty and telling them to meet up with him at the park as well. The fine mist that had started this morning was now a downpour. Sheriff Ourso stood under a pavilion near the entrance to the park and helped the park ranger arrange the search and rescue teams. They would have to split up to cover the area. Due to the rain, the dogs wouldn't be of any help right now, if at all. The vehicles would be towed back to the Sheriff's Department where techs were waiting to process them. He was expecting the same results as Dylan's car, no prints and no clues as to their whereabouts.

***

The cool morning air awoke Barbara with a startle. The air was ripe with the damp scent of the wet ground from last night's rain and the stench of the pig manure. The moan of the wind blowing through the old barn sent goose bumps up and down her body. From the corner of her eye, she caught a glimpse of movement from the doorway. Their tormentors were back. She froze in fear. Why were they playing these games with them? Death would be welcomed.

Her heart beat wildly against her chest. Who would they humiliate and torture this time? Her throat seemed to close up on her. She had a hard time catching her breath. *Get a grip girl, now was not the time to have a panic attack.* These two were homicidal maniacs and she needed to keep her head on straight, if she wanted to escape.

All of a sudden, one of her captors appeared in front of her. His creepy eyes stared down at her. She tried desperately to swallow back the spine-chilling fear bubbling up inside her. She knew it was her turn.

Without hesitation, the knife slipped into her skin. Her voice became hoarse from her screams. He could see the dread in her eyes. The pain became too much for her and she passed out. However, the man wasn't done with this one and revived her.

***

David pulled out his journal to update today's entries.

Macabre Torture Journal

Length of time it takes for antifreeze to kill subject – Test subject Michael has had small amounts of antifreeze added to his water. Antifreeze is taking a long time to show any serious side effects, dosage increased. Psychological torture is working well though – does not take any joy in watching wife being raped.

Length of time it takes for rat poison to kill the subject. Test subject Barbara is being submitted to this torture currently while being tortured in various other ways with knives and burns, as well as rape.

Is it possible to stretch a subject to death? Test subject Heather has been stretched even more. More discomfort noticed from being stretched. Very little fight left in her.

Acupuncture using long hot needles – slowly add burning candles to needles. Test subject Jill has four needles inserted into her, one in each arm and leg. Candles placed on the needles and lit. The wax dripping down causes discomfort. Test subject Jill screamed louder when being raped, possibly to make husband suffer?

Bury subject where only head was exposed and remove eyelids – let ants and bugs finish off. Test subject Dylan has succumbed to death. Fed to pigs.

Make a small incision in gut to pull out the intestines. Restrain subject for animals to munch on. Test subject Randy has been restrained to a stall right at the entrance of the barn. Test subject Barbara is restrained in the cell next to boyfriend for maximum benefit

Now that Dylan had succumbed to his tortures, David thought it was time to share his latest accomplishment with Sheriff Hamilton. It had been a while since he had sent her an actual memento from his kills and he didn't want her to think he had given up his hobby. Since there wasn't much left of Dylan, he would have to send the good Sheriff some of Dylan's teeth. The bugs did quite a number on Dylan.

The Traveler was glad Dylan suffered as long as he did. "It's going to be just as much fun feeding him to the pigs." The Traveler was sweaty and tired. It took both men to load Dylan's body into the wood chipper to feed to the pigs. Afterwards, they made sure everything was clean and ready for the next time.

Chapter 28

 The streets of Lake Hamilton were devoid of life tonight. The recent disappearances were wearing on the townspeople's nerves. No one knew what had happened to some of their prominent members, but they were disappearing into thin air and never heard from again. There had been no bank or cell phone activity. Most of their cars had vanished along with them. To date, no bodies had been found. It was as if they fell off the face of the earth. Where the hell could these people be? Everyone seemed to be more aware of what was happening around them. Patrols had been stepped up. A strange person or vehicle in town created anxious calls into the sheriff's office, keeping the officers busier than normal.

Sheriff Ourso reached for a cigarette, as a chill went through his body. He couldn't shake the feeling that the town was being watched by an unforeseen force. Something sinister was closing in on this small town. Evil lurked in the shadows.

***

Hannah Easley fell in love with her latest jewelry design. The pink sapphire dome ring was breathtaking. What had started out as a hobby to keep her from losing her mind from boredom, has turned into a lucrative business. Hannah started out as a bored housewife and ended up a middle aged divorcee, whose life had been completely turned upside down. It all worked out in the end, though, and she even managed to land on her own feet; that was if she could feel those feet.

At the age of 30, Hannah started noticing a few mysterious ailments, and two years later she was diagnosed with Multiple Sclerosis. Her husband, Doug Fisher, decided that he couldn't handle being married to a handicapped woman and left her for someone that was much younger. As luck would have it, he was the one that ended up with egg on his face. The younger woman ended up leaving Doug for a man more her age.

At first, Hannah had a hard time dealing with her disability and divorce at the same time, but she had learned how to cope with the ups and downs of multiple sclerosis - and single life couldn't be better. She had even met a wonderful man that didn't mind the fact that she had an incurable disease, with symptoms that were as mysterious as the disease itself. Hannah never knew what problems she would encounter from one day to the next, but she refused to let the illness define her. She would fight it with every molecule she had in her body.

Frank Ourso was the best thing that had ever happened to her. He helped her keep her sanity. As she looked out her jewelry shop window, she smiled. Speaking of the devil, he was coming her way.

"Hey handsome, I was just thinking about you."

Frank still couldn't believe how lucky he was to have Hannah in his life. She kept him grounded. "How's it going over here?"

"It's been pretty steady. The internet sales are up by ten percent, which is always a good thing. I just completed the pink sapphire ring and absolutely love it. I can't wait to get it photographed and on the website. I have a feeling it will sell like hot cakes."

"That's good, but you aren't overdoing it, are you?"

"No, Dr. Ourso, I'm not." Hannah jokingly stated. She did, however, like that he took the time to concern himself with how she was feeling. It was kind of nice to have someone baby her.

"I can't help but worry about you."

"I'm fine. I've learned how to pace myself and trust me, I don't want to deliberately bring on an exacerbation of my symptoms. I'm looking forward to spending some time alone with you."

Frank gave her a devilish smile, "I can't wait to get you alone tonight and give you a preview of what's to come." That statement alone brought a twinkle to Hannah's eyes.

Frank and Hannah had been planning a getaway trip for a couple of months now. They were going to spend a weekend over in Virginia Beach, Virginia. They needed some time away from the prying eyes of the town. Plus, there was a jewelry expo this weekend that Hannah wanted to go to.

"Frank, have you noticed the stranger in town? I've seen him a few times over the last several weeks. I'm not sure where he is staying, but I swear he looks familiar. I just can't put a name to the face. My memory is so bad lately."

"No, I'm sorry, I haven't."

Hannah knew his face looked familiar, but she just couldn't place it. That was one of the worst side effects from this blasted disease - the memory problems. She had been so bad with names lately.

"I'll be on the lookout for him. If you see him, you can always give me a call. Where have you noticed him? I can swing by and see if they know anything."

"I think he has been at the hardware store, but I honestly haven't paid that much attention. I want to say he drives a big old motor home."

"Well, there you go. That is most probably where he is staying. More than likely he is someone camping at one of the local parks."

"I guess you're right."

"You guess? I am always right."

"I'm ready to close up for the night. You want to take me home? I can get my car tomorrow."

On the ride over to Hannah's house, she could tell he was thinking about the disappearances. She could see the worry etched on his face.

As they walked into the house, he expressed his frustration. "What the hell is going on in this town, Hannah? Where are all these people? I don't see Dylan walking away from the car dealership."

Hannah slowly walked up to Frank. Frank framed Hannah's face with his hands and kissed her deeply, passionately. Hannah slid her hands up and down Frank's chest. She was impatient to feel his bare skin against hers. The raw desire overpowered all her senses. Frank's kisses turned hotter, hungrier. He pushed her dress off her shoulders in one sweep. Next went her bra.

He gently cupped her breasts in his hands, rubbing the rosy nipples, watching them harden with his touch. Desire coursed through Hannah. Laying her down on the bed, he took one rosebud in his mouth and suckled, teasing her. The sensation was instantly electrifying. A moan escaped Hannah. Hannah pulled Frank closer. Her need for Frank burned hot inside her. Hannah gasped in delight, as Frank trailed kisses lower and lower down her body. She began to lose complete control. She reached out and touched him, savoring the hardness of him. He was so hot and hard, she could feel him pulsating with her touch.

"You are killing me. I can't take anymore." In one swift moment, he was inside her, filling her completely. She rode him, taking each thrust deeper and deeper into her being. Hannah screamed out as a wave of climaxes engulfed her. All those years of her ex-husband telling her how she was ice cold in bed, and had no passion, was so wrong. He just didn't know how to please her. Frank made her feel like a woman should. Hannah felt him shudder deep inside of her and she knew she had satisfied him as well. Curling up beside him, she fell asleep, happier than she had been in a very long time. She was amazed that her life felt so perfect. He made her feel whole again. After her divorce, she had sworn off men, never thinking someone or something was missing in her life.

Hannah listened to Frank sleep. She didn't want to wake him up and carefully eased herself out of bed. The pain was just too bad to lie in bed. Being quiet, she went into the kitchen to fix her a cup of tea and a piece of toast. If she had something in her stomach, she could at least take a pain pill. Maybe then she would get some much needed rest.

She brewed herself a cup of chamomile tea and took it into the living room. She'd bought a new book last week and hadn't found the time to read it yet. Maybe between the tea, pain pill, and book she could relax enough to sleep. Hannah didn't understand why the pain had to be so bad at night time. At least during the day it was bearable, but come bedtime, she couldn't seem to get comfortable anymore.

Chapter 29

Joanne Harmon had enjoyed cooking since she was eight years old. She had always wanted to be a chef and open her own restaurant. Looking around, she couldn't believe that dream was becoming a reality. She was taking a huge chance on naming the restaurant "Harmony", but it seemed to fit. She couldn't wait to open the doors and see how everyone loved her food. This would either make or break her.

She wanted this restaurant to be a place where friends came to meet over good food and wine. Joanne was certain she had created the perfect ambiance for it.

Joanne walked into the kitchen to make sure everything was arranged for the sous chefs. She had left note cards explaining the entire menu items in detail, in case someone forgot how a menu item was made. It may take them a while to catch on to the recipes. Her cooking was considered nouveau American. She had a flare with food, per her culinary instructor. Hopefully the customers thought so too.

Joanne couldn't believe how well opening night went. The restaurant was a huge success. All throughout dinner service she heard oh's, ah's, and mm's. People seemed to enjoy the food.

Joanne wanted to do a final walk through to make sure everything was picked up and turned off before going home for the night. A noise out back caught her attention. A tinge of fear ran through her body, no one should be out back at this hour. Thankfully, she had listened to the insurance salesman and installed video cameras. Joanne looked at the feed to see who was out there. It had to be a cat. The reason she came back to Lake Hamilton was the lack of crime. Installing the video camera system had seemed silly, but it did drop her premiums.

Joanne noticed an old truck parked out back. A guy seemed to be loading something quite large into the bed of his truck. As if he felt Joanne looking at him, he suddenly looked around.

Joanne ducked away from the camera, not thinking. *You silly woman he can't see you in here.* She could hear her own rapid heart rate caused by the sudden rush of fear. Swallowing back her fear, she called the sheriff's office.

"This is Joanne Harmon. I'm over at Harmony and wanted to let you know that something strange is going on around back. A guy, no wait, two guys are loading something large into the back of a truck. Oh my God, it's a person, maybe a body."

"Ms. Harmon, are you somewhere safe? Can they see or hear you?"

"I'm inside my restaurant watching them, they have no idea."

"I'm sending help right now. Please, don't go outside. The police car will go in silent, as not to scare them away."

"Well, they better hurry, because it looks like they are pulling out right now."

***

The Traveler didn't like the way the old geezer kept staring at him. "Son, are you from around here?"

Uh-oh. The Traveler knew it might cause a problem coming into town so much. "No sir, just passing through."

"You sure do look familiar."

The Traveler and David had just managed to load up Mr. Jerry Kirshman and everything they needed from the hardware store, when the police cruiser passed them. They had just pulled out of the alleyway when he noticed the cruiser turning into the alley between the restaurant and hardware store.

"What the hell?" The Traveler muttered to himself. He knew no one was around when they grabbed the old coot. The damn old man had finally recognized him. They fixed that problem, though. The old goat would probably have a heart attack before they even got him to the hideout. At least they went unnoticed by the cop.

Several nights later, David and The Traveler decided to treat themselves to a beer in a local bar a few towns over. A reward was well deserved for all they had accomplished so far.

The Traveler froze; on the TV he saw a news crew in front of the hardware store in Lake Hamilton. "Hey bartender, can you turn it up a minute."

The news reporter was pointing towards the alley, "Law enforcement agencies here in Lake Hamilton are asking anyone with information regarding the disappearance of Jerry Kirshman, to please contact them. A witness noticed a late model Dodge truck, gray in color, leaving the alleyway Tuesday night. The owner of the vehicle is not a suspect, but may have seen something that can help authorities locate Mr. Kirshman.

"Mr. Kirshman is 79 years old and has owned Kirshman Hardware since 1963. The locals here can't think of anyone who would want to cause him harm."

It was all The Traveler could do to keep from spewing his beer all over the bar. Who the hell had been in the alley to see them? The bartender glanced over at him, "You know the old man?"

"Nope. That reporter looked familiar. She's hot."

Chapter 30

Sheriff Hamilton eyed the envelope waiting for her on her desk. It had been a while since she'd received something from David Thorguson. With it being in a small envelope, it couldn't be anything too bad, or she hoped at least. Folded up inside the note were four teeth. The note simply asked, "Did you miss me?" That was easy for her to answer – no.

She called Alex before calling Agent O'Riordan. "I thought you might like to know I received another package from David Thorguson."

"I'll be right over."

"It's all right. It was teeth. He wanted to know if I missed him, as if. I'm getting ready to call Agent O'Riordan and inform him."

"I wish you would have called to let me know. I would have been there for you."

"I know. I will see you at lunch. I love you."

"I love you, too."

Sheriff Hamilton called Agent O'Riordan next. "Agent O'Riordan, its Sheriff Hamilton. I thought you might like to know I received a package from David Thorguson today. It contained teeth and a note. The package was mailed from West Virginia."

"I was right; he was headed to West Virginia then. I haven't received any hits on VICAP, though. I'll have Agent Manning double check. Maybe someone didn't enter it into VICAP or the body has yet to be discovered. At least we know where he has been; now to figure out where they are going next. Thanks for the call, Sheriff; I'll send someone over to pick up everything from you. Maybe we can get some DNA from the teeth and search through missing persons."

"I'll have it waiting at the front desk."

***

Agent O'Riordan wondered why David Thorguson and his accomplice had been so quiet. What were they up to?

O'Riordan couldn't remember the last time he actually had a good night's sleep. All he did lately was toss and turn. He had reviewed the files so much, that he knew them backwards and forward. What were they missing? He had been trying to map out their path, but with no bodies showing up, it was impossible. Even David Thorguson rarely sent Sheriff Hamilton his little packages of mementos. Did this mean there were no new bodies and they had stopped for now? He hoped that this was the case, but he feared it was something much worse.

O'Riordan let his thoughts drift to Meghan. Even though they had only known each other a brief period of time, she had him thinking of trying marriage again, even a kid or two. They had never even talked about what would happen to their relationship once this case was settled, but it was at the top of his list. He didn't want to stop seeing her - of that he was certain.

Chapter 31

Adele Fisher fell madly in love with her husband Stephen in high school. That love never faded while he was away for four years in the Air Force.

During high school, Adele never missed a home football game. Watching him play always made her beam with pride. When he was away in the Air Force, she couldn't wait for his visits back home. They married not long after he returned home for good. It had been blissful happiness since they said "I do".

As she looked outside from the kitchen window, a shiver of fear snaked down her spine. The stillness of the night was eerily peaceful, a peacefulness that would soon be taken over by pure evil.

Adele's nerves were strung tight tonight, but she swore she could feel a predator's eyes upon her, watching her every move. Stop it! Just because prominent members of this town were vanishing into thin air didn't mean she had to let paranoia overcome her. She was just anxious for Steve to come home from work. She hated when he worked late, but with Michael Redmond still missing, he had to help pick up the slack.

Shaking off the feelings overpowering her mind, she walked upstairs. As she settled in bed, the hairs on the back of her neck rose. Someone was in the house, and

she didn't hear the garage door open. She could
barely make out the noise, but it sounded as if
footsteps were coming up the stairs. Before she could
lock the bedroom door, a man appeared in the
doorway. Strong arms pinned her to the bed while he
clamped a rag over her mouth and forced her to
breath in the drug.

***

The feeling of being extremely cold woke Adele. A chill
ran through her body. Something wasn't right. Her
mouth felt as if it were full of cotton and she was so
damned thirsty.

Adele carefully opened her eyes. She fought back
dizziness and nausea. Darkness surrounded her. She
couldn't see a thing. She started to panic. She was
deathly afraid of the dark. She reminded herself to
stay calm; panicking wouldn't help her.

A foul odor penetrated her senses. It smelled rotten,
almost like something was decaying .

As her eyes came into focus, she observed her
surroundings with grim determination. Most of her
friends were here, caged like animals. Fear rushed
through her body. She had difficulty breathing. She
could feel a thin wire around her neck tighten, when
she tried to move even a fraction. Her lungs burned
with every breath she took, pain seared through her
body. Fear gripped its icy cold grasp around her. She

forced herself to breath slowly. A sense of hopelessness took over. She had to get her emotions under control. Hysteria would do her no good.

The psychotic demon that approached her looked so familiar. Whatever he had in mind, she knew it wasn't good. She was not ready to die. If only she could wake up from this nightmare. Who the hell was this man?

When she flinched from his touch, the cold hard steel of the restraints bit into her skin. The pain was excruciating.

"I thought it was time for you to join your friends, you little bitch. My collection is almost complete." Her captor's eyes glistened with a deep-seated hatred. Pure evil twisted his lips into a snarl. "I thought for sure I would have trouble rounding your little group up, but no, you all stayed in this godforsaken town. What's wrong? No one had dreams of moving away, or is it because you knew that anywhere else you would be just another face in the crowd?"

She tried to remember who this man was. Cutting through the haze and confusion fogging up her brain was nearly impossible. He looked so familiar, but she couldn't put a name to the face.

"I bet you all thought I would never be back in town after the torment you put me through. Well, I'm back, and now it's my turn to torment you and your friends."

His raspy voice sounded like fingernails scraping across a chalkboard.

She barely had enough moisture left in her mouth to moisten her chapped, cracked lips. "Who are you?"

"You will remember me soon enough. I'm sure your friends will tell you who I am. Just remember, now I am the one in power."

Her mind was reeling now. Why couldn't she place him? Sudden realization hit her like a ton of bricks. Their tormentor couldn't be him. She looked at him, his movements. She was almost positive it was him. The earth seemed to shift beneath her feet. They were all doomed.

From the corner of her eye, she noticed another man moving closer. She tried desperately to escape. The wire around her neck prevented her from making anything but slight movements.

Her tormentor let the knife blade tickle her skin. She tried to squirm away from the tip. Ever so gently, the blade slid into the skin of her belly. She screamed in agony. He moved up to her nipples and traced them with the blade, slowly drawing blood. He let the blade tease her. Next, David moved on to the branding iron he had heating. She felt the heat radiate off the metal before it ever touched her flesh. Once it made contact, the pain was instantaneous and took her breath away. The air smelled of burning flesh and blood.

She shuddered in fear as the other man moved closer to her with a fire extinguisher in his hands. In a surreal moment, she watched as he took expert precision and sprayed a short blast at her feet with the foaming retardant. The cold immediately seeped into her body.

The Traveler told her, "It is time for you all to pay for your sins."

Mascara streaked down her cheeks, mixing with her tears. "Please, let me go. We were just kids!" Her smeared scarlet red lipstick reminded him of a clown.

She pulled harder on the bindings, screaming in terror and agony, as he repeatedly sprayed a fire extinguisher on her foot and leg. "Help, please, someone help me."

"Scream all you want. No one can help you or your friends. There is no one around to hear your screams." Anger flickered in his eyes.

When she noticed the saw in his hand, she tried desperately to free herself. She watched in horror, as he cut off the leg he had sprayed. "You know, I've always heard that phantom pain is just as bad as real pain. I decided to test that theory on you." Her screams turned into howls of anguish. It reminded him of a wounded animal that knew it was about to die. His erection grew even harder as he used the glowing hot brand to cauterize the stump before she bled to death.

She felt the darkness overcoming her and welcomed the black abyss of unconsciousness.

Macabre Torture Journal

Length of time it takes for antifreeze to kill subject – Test subject Michael has had increased amounts of antifreeze added to his water. Severe discomfort noted. Psychological torture worked better with each rape of his wife. The wife no longer looks to him for help.

Length of time it takes rat poison to kill the subject. Test subject Barbara is being submitted to this torture. Poison was increased as it is slow to cause discomfort.

Does Phantom pain exist – removal of a limb from subject (Must cauterize to keep said subject from bleeding to death) Test subject Adele had her left leg amputated just below knee.

Is it possible to stretch a subject to death? Test subject Heather has been stretched even more. Severe discomfort noticed from being stretched. No fight left in her.

Acupuncture using long hot needles – slowly add burning candles to needles. Test subject Jill has six needles inserted into her, one in each breast, arm and leg. Candles placed on the needles and lit. The wax dripping down causes discomfort. Test subject Jill screamed louder while being raped, possibly to make husband suffer.

Make a small incision in gut to pull out the intestines. Restrain subject for animals to munch on. Test subject Randy has been restrained to a stall right at the entrance of the barn. Test subject Barbara is restrained in the cell next to boyfriend for maximum benefit. Rats feeding off of test subject very slowly. Extreme discomfort noted.

Suspend subject above bamboo shoots and wait for them to grow into test subject. Test subject Maria has been chosen for this torture. Bamboo has started to grow, not too much longer before it reaches her.

Chapter 32

Steve Fisher was finally home. It had been a long work week, but today had been especially long. Mr. Redmond was worried about Michael and Jill. Neither had been heard from or seen since their disappearance. He was even talking about hiring a private investigator to look into their disappearance. Shit, even Steve was worried. Michael would never walk away from the practice. He was the one that convinced Steve into going to college, to become a lawyer after the military. Not that Steve regretted it. The military gave him some real world experience, but he didn't want to do manual labor for a living. Although, Steve must admit, practicing law could sometimes be mundane. It seemed as if lately all they did was frivolous lawsuits and wills. It paid the bills, though, and he wasn't sweating his ass off. Making good money was nice also. Steve grew up with a silver spoon in his mouth, but he wouldn't see any of his parents' money until they died. Even that wouldn't be anytime soon, the old codger was too mean to die. Steve never had a desire to follow in his father's footsteps

When Steve walked into the house from the garage, he knew something was wrong. The house had a strange odor to it, reminiscent of old sweat, and the back door was ajar. He called for Adele and when she didn't answer, Steve became concerned. After searching the house for her, he called 911.

The nighttime dispatcher answered the phone. "This is Steve Fisher. I just came home and my back door was jimmied open. I can't find my wife Adele anywhere."

The dispatcher asked him to stay on the line while she dispatched a unit out to his house and called Sheriff Ourso.

***

Sheriff Frank Ourso knew something was wrong, when dispatch called. "Sheriff speaking ."

"Sir, we just got a call from Steve Fisher. It looks as if someone broke into his house and his wife is missing."

"I'm on my way over. Please have Detectives Brown and Laughlin meet me there. They are leading the other missing person's investigations. We need the crime scene techs over there as well. Have them dust for fingerprints and check in with the neighbors to see if they saw anything out of the ordinary. Somebody has to have seen something."

"Yes, sir, I'll get right on it."

It didn't appear to be a robbery, but the scene was similar to the other missing citizen's homes. So far, the main things taken from the residences were food, gas, and miscellaneous tools. What was going on around here and where were all these people? No bodies had shown up, but no activity had been detected from the checking accounts or cell phones. Hell, some cell phones had been left in the houses. Michael Redmond's car was missing from the house, but whoever stole the car knew how to dismantle the Lojack.

* * *

Steve didn't believe that Adele would leave him. They had been planning a big vacation, both wanting to get away for a little bit. Adele had always wanted to see Italy and he finally convinced her to take a cruise around the Mediterranean. The ports of call were all places Adele had wanted to visit, including Spain and Italy.

Too worried to sleep, Steven answered the phone on the first ring, hoping it was Adele. "Do you miss your wife? It's time you did penance for your sins."

Steve couldn't place the voice. "Who is this? Where is Adele? What have you done with her?"

"It's time for you and your friends to pay."

"What do you mean pay? Who is this? Do you know where everyone is? What is going on? I'll pay any ransom amount to have her back. Please!"

"You will soon find out who this is. You haven't suffered enough yet."

Shit, the caller hung up, before Steve could get any information out of him. He called Sheriff Ourso right away, "Sheriff, I know it's late, but I just had a strange phone call. The caller asked if I missed my wife and said that I would pay. Actually, he said me and my friends would pay for our sins."

"Okay, let me get someone over there right away and put a trace on your phone. If he calls again, we will be ready. I will see if the phone company has a record of the call and can get me the number."

"Caller ID showed unlisted."

"We may be able to get more information from the telephone company. I might not be able to get in touch with anyone until morning, though."

Steve couldn't help but worry. Pay, pay for what? Who did he piss off, and why were his friends involved? Did this have something to do with the others going missing? No one else had received a phone call that he knew of.

With tears running down his face, he dropped to his knees and prayed that Adele was ok. This had to be a cruel joke. He couldn't think of anyone who wanted to hurt Adele. Where was she?

***

Sheriff Ourso didn't like what was going on around this town. This was the first time someone had received any type of communication since a family member or friend had disappeared. What did the person mean by pay for their sins? These were all upstanding citizens of the town. What dirty little secret were they hiding that could cause them to disappear? It was time to interview the families again, and question them a little harder, to see if someone could have a personal vendetta against the missing people. He needed to find out a little more about their lives.

Chapter 33

A row of tall, dense oleander trees separated the bar
from the shopping center. The Traveler assumed the
shopping center owner didn't want his shoppers
having to worry about the patrons of the bar. The
oleanders also offered the perfect cover, while he
watched and waited for the opportune moment to
strike. The inky blackness of the night allowed him to
lurk in the shadows unnoticed.

He knew Chuck Anderson would be leaving the bar
soon. Of course, Chuck wouldn't be caught dead in a
bar in his own home town. The Traveler got lucky one
day and noticed him come into this one.

The Traveler and David had taken a chance one night
and disguised themselves so they could enjoy a night
on the town. David craved the exhilaration of a hunt.
Waiting in the motor home didn't offer the same rush.
It turned out to be a wise move. The Traveler
recognized Chuck right away. They scoped out the
place and confirmed this was a habit with good ole
Chuck. Of course, David didn't allow those Friday
nights to be wasted trips. Several women made it back
to the workshop for David to take out his aggression
on before feeding them to the pigs. Their pigs were
the biggest in all of West Virginia. They had rounded
up several more over the last few months. The

Traveler had sold three at the slaughterhouse in Berkshire for a nice profit.

He had learned from the old coot at the hardware store that his parents had died several years back. The Traveler didn't even think twice about his parents' deaths. There was no love lost there. Even if he had known, he wouldn't have come back.

Selling the pigs to the slaughterhouse had been a risk worth taking. The old man there wouldn't tell anyone he was back in town, besides he couldn't care less. He probably didn't even know The Traveler had left Lake Hamilton years ago. The Traveler was certain he didn't know where the pigs were raised. It had always been a cash only basis. He never asked his dad questions when he brought in pigs to sell for butchering. Most of the pigs his dad brought to the slaughterhouse were "strays" that wandered onto the farm.

The Traveler couldn't believe they managed to abduct Chuck as easily as they did. It had been easy to slip a roofie into Chuck's drink at the bar.

***

The first thing Chuck noticed when he woke up was the putrid smell. Where was it coming from? He blinked several times to clear his vision.

He tried to sit up but couldn't move. His feet and hands were restrained. What the hell was going on?

Apprehension rose up inside of him. He tried pulling harder on the restraints to free himself.

The repugnant smell reminded him of something dead or rotting. Come on, Chuck, wake up. This was just a nightmare. You are hung over, that's all. The white hot pain confirmed that this wasn't a dream. He tried to remember what happened to him. The last thing he could recall was sitting in a bar drinking.

"Chuck, I didn't think you would ever wake up. I've dreamed about this for so long. The first thing I plan to do is take your manhood away from you."

Chuck heard the voice speaking to him from out of the darkness, but he couldn't believe his ears. He pulled even harder on the restraints.

"Oh, don't worry, Chuck. I'm not going to cut it off. I have something far better planned." The Traveler picked up the super glue and laughed when Chuck's eyes almost bulged out in terror.

"You see, Chuck, super glue does even more damage than a knife. Besides, I don't want you to bleed to death right away, there would be no fun in that."

Chuck heard moaning and weeping. "Where am I? Who else is here? What is going on?"

"Don't worry, Chuck, your friends are here with you. It's time you all paid for tormenting me."

Dread coiled through Chuck's body. Who was this maniac? "Who are you?"

His tormentor's dark gaze narrowed, "You will remember me soon enough. You and your friends don't deserve to live. Death is too good for you. You must suffer first."

Chuck's voice shook with fear. There had to be some way out of this. "Let me go. I can pay you."

"Chuck, your money means nothing to me. It's time that you suffered the same way I suffered. Well, maybe you will suffer a little more than me."

"What do you mean suffer? What are you planning on doing to me?" Even though Chuck asked, he wasn't sure he wanted to know the answer.

"You will soon find out, all in due time."

"You won't get away with this. People are already talking about the disappearances around town. Someone will come looking for us." Chuck tried once again to free himself from the restraints, pulling even harder this time. The restraints refused to break.

"Your friends have also begged and pleaded for their lives, but it has done them no good either. I am the one in control now and there is nothing you can do about it."

The smell of death hung heavy in the air. He knew some of his friends may have already died here. Who was this guy?   What did he ever do to this maniac?

Chuck lost track of time. He no longer knew how long he had been here. Most of the others had grown silent, some let out pitiful moans. Chuck wasn't ready to die, especially not in this hell hole.

The restraints had rubbed his wrists and ankles raw. Now every time he moved, the wounds would start to bleed again. He went beyond hunger and thirst. What water they had been given was dirty and foul smelling.

The Traveler leered at him and told him, "Chuck, my old friend, I think it's about time you learn what it feels like to have ashes flicked at you.”

Chuck had noticed a small, contained fire being started in the barrel. He watched in horror as his tormentor fanned the hot embers across his body. As they landed on him, he felt the never ending sting.

Chuck tried to move away from the hot ashes as much as he could. Still, they managed to land on most of his body, searing into his skin. He shrieked from the pain. "Man, you are crazy! Let us go, you freak. You were a wimp then and a wimp now. You have to keep us restrained to do your bidding. What's wrong? Are you afraid that without the restraints we would beat you in your own game?"

A cruel sneer formed across his tormentor's face as he picked up a sledgehammer and struck Chuck's leg with tremendous force. You could hear the bone splintering, as the skin was ripped away from his leg.

Red-hot pain tore through Chuck's body. He had never endured such agony. His whole body seemed to vibrate viciously. Raw tears escaped from his eyes. His tormentor had a fiendish glare in his eyes now. He watched in horror as the man picked up the sledgehammer once again and took a blow at the other leg. The pain became too much and his world went black.

Through the veil of darkness, he heard his tormentor speaking to him, his voice now feral, "I still haven't shown you just how demented I am."

Through glazed eyes, he watched his tormentor stoke the embers again. Chuck knew his death was close at hand.

The Traveler used a pair of tongs to pick up one of the hot coals and walked towards Chuck. "Come on, Chuck. I have a special cocktail for you to drink."

Chuck had hoped he wouldn't wake up again, that death was finally coming for him, but he was wrong.

Macabre Torture Journal

Length of time it takes for antifreeze to kill subject – Test subject Michael succumbed to the antifreeze. Fed to pigs.

Length of time it takes for rat poison to kill the subject- Test subject Barbara -Poison increased – more discomfort noticed.

Does phantom pain truly exist – removal of a limb from subject (Must cauterize to keep said subject from bleeding to death) Test subject Adele had her left leg amputated just below knee. Subject constantly cries out in pain and is incoherent most of the time. Still responds to rape and torture.

What happens when the subject ingests lighter fluid, and is then forced to swallow hot coals? Test subject Chuck fought drinking lighter fluid. Several coals ingested and howled in pain.

Is it possible to stretch a subject to death? Test subject Heather has been stretched even more. Severe discomfort noticed from being stretched. No fight left in her.

Acupuncture using long hot needles – slowly add burning candles to needles. Test subject Jill has 12 needles inserted into her now; two in each breast, arm and leg. Candles placed on the needles and lit. Test subject Jill no longer responsive to rape.

Make a small incision in gut to pull out the intestines. Restrain subject for animals to munch on. Extreme discomfort noted. Test subject Randy barely hanging on.

Suspend subject above bamboo shoots and wait for them to grow into the subject. Test subject Maria has been chosen for this torture. Bamboo is starting to touch the body.

***

Chloe Hatfield was starting to panic. She had tried to call Chuck on his cell phone, at home, the country club, and even the bar he frequented with no luck. He didn't answer his cell or home phone and neither the country club nor bar had seen him. She had left several messages, but as of yet he still hadn't called her back. Both of them had been worried about the disappearances of their friends and thought it was best to keep in touch. She was trying to keep from becoming hysterical, but with all the disappearances, it was hard not to. Where the hell could he be?

***

Sheriff Hamilton saw the federal express driver as she was leaving her office for lunch. A chill crept down her spine. It was a visceral reaction now that David Thorguson had taken up sending her packages again, she wasn't sure if she wanted to know who it was from or what was in the box for that matter.

She called Alex, "I received another package. Did you want to meet me here instead of at the restaurant? It's a large package and I don't want to be the one to open it."

"I'll be there shortly. I'll call Agent O'Riordan and inform him also."

"I can do that. I just don't want to see what is inside."

Sheriff Hamilton called Agent O'Riordan, "I received another package from David Thorguson. Alex is on his way over to see what's inside, but you should know the package was sent from West Virginia again."

"I'm anxious to see what is inside. We still have had no hits from VICAP on murders matching our MO or signatures, so either the bodies aren't being found, or they're not being input into VICAP. It's interesting that the packages are still coming from West Virginia. Did it come from the same city again?"

"No, it was sent from a different city, but still West Virginia. Alex just arrived, so hold on and you can find out what was mailed."

"Okay."

Alex knew from the weight that it was something larger than teeth, nails or eyes. Nestled inside the box was a heart with a note, "The poor man's heart just wasn't in it".

Alex took the phone from Jordan, "O'Riordan, he mailed a heart this time."

"I'll send someone over to pick it up; now to find out who the latest victim was and why no murders have been reported yet." Agent O'Riordan wondered where David Thorguson and his accomplice were. Suddenly, the bodies were no longer being discovered. Why were they being careful disposing of them now?

Chapter 34

She hated being caged like an animal. She always knew this guy had a screw loose. On top of that, it was pitch black in here. She heard the others moving around in an attempt to find some comfort from their restraints.

With each passing day she became more sluggish, growing weaker. Her mind and body were fatigued beyond the point of return now; all she wanted to do was close her eyes and sleep. The foul and fetid odor that surrounded her no longer bothered her. Her eyelids grew heavier by the minute. Maybe she would fall asleep and never wake up from this nightmare. She had lost count as to how many days she had been here. How long did he plan to keep them all caged here?

The wind blowing through the rafters wreaked havoc on her nerves and the moonlight cast foreboding shadows that danced across the old barn. She heard a distinct rustling near the doorway and this time it wasn't the wind. Squinting into the darkness, she tried to make out what the noise was. Was that footsteps she heard? Were the crazy maniacs back? The hairs on the back of her neck stood up. They were back. What horrendous torture did they have planned tonight?

She heard another sound. The pigs outside began to make noise, their incessant squealing grated on her nerves. Even the pigs seemed to sense the evil that surrounded their captors, it seeped from their very pores.

A fire had been started in the middle of the room. Whatever they had planned must involve fire.   The smell of burning flesh reached her nose, causing her to gag. She couldn't help but scream. She heard the others starting to panic as well. Their screams didn't bother the tormentors. The louder the screams, the worse the torture became. This was what he wanted, to terrorize them the way he felt they terrorized him all those years ago. The screams echoed in the barn, wearing on her nerves. If only she could cover her ears and drown it out. Sweat clung to her skin, drawing the bugs to her. She could feel them biting into her exposed body. If only she could swipe them away, or at least scratch the places they had bitten. The constant itching drove her crazy.

At times, the eerie silence was worse than the terrifying screams. The smell of burning flesh became stronger, causing her to dry heave. She couldn't remember the last time she'd had something to eat. All that had been provided to them was dirty, foul smelling water.

Their captors continued to laugh while tormenting Chuck. Over the flame, she made out the cruel, menacing stare of their other captor. This one was pure evil. Fear curdled inside of her as she watched the glee in his eyes. She tried to scramble closer to the wall as he headed her way. The lunatic was coming for her.

David grabbed her by the hair and forced her to look up at him. In the background, she heard the flames sizzling and popping. "I think I'll have my fun with you for now."

A sickening clarity settled in her sluggish brain. This was her last few moments on this earth and they would not be pleasant. Sheer terror pierced through her body, too weak to fight and scream, she accepted her fate for what it was.

These last few days had been hell on earth, the worst nightmare possible. Pain had been her constant reminder that she was not dreaming, but living this nightmare. If she thought she had experienced excruciating pain over the last few days, it was nothing compared to what she was experiencing right now. Raw pain gripped her face as he forced something in her nasal cavity. She felt the warm blood oozing down her face, some making its way down her throat and choking her. When the pain became unbearable, she welcomed the darkness. This would be her last breath, but she was ready for death to take her away.

* * *

David had been intrigued with the mummification process ever since his parents took him to see the King Tut Exhibit. Looking over the crude instruments they found in the old barn, he realized this might be the perfect time to experiment with some of the rituals performed for mummification. Of course, his victim would need to be alive for the beginning of the process. He had always been fascinated with how they removed the brain from the nose. Now to find out if that was possible.

David dragged her to a table he had set up with several sets of restraints. As weak as she seemed to be, it was imperative he keep her as still as possible. He knew instinct would take over once he began and she would try to move away from the instruments. Anticipation hummed through his body as he prepared her for mummification.

"You are in for a special treat today. Do you know anything about ancient Egypt and how they would mummify the remains? I've always been intrigued by this and have decided to try a few of their techniques. However, it wouldn't be as much fun to do this on an already dead person. I can't wait to find out if the brains really do come out of the nose liquefied."

He could smell the fear in the air. Fear was a powerful drug to him, one he was desperately addicted to.

Before performing the mummification process on said subject, David cut out her tongue. This would be a nice little memento to send to his sweet sheriff.

David watched in awe as she started convulsing, her legs and arms jittered wildly. Her eyes rolled back into her head and then her whole body became stiff. He watched the brain matter ooze from her nose and flow down her body. It was a bigger thrill than he expected. While her body was still warm and before his friend used the super glue on her, he found his release.

Macabre Torture Journal

Mummification – while the subject is alive. Test subject Heather has been chosen for this, as she no longer shows emotion when raped.

Length of time it took for rat poison to kill the subject. Test subject Barbara was being submitted to this torture. Poison increased – more discomfort noticed.

Does phantom pain truly exist – removal of a limb from subject (Must cauterize to keep said subject from bleeding to death) Test subject Adele had her left leg amputated just below knee. Subject bleary eyed and in constant pain.

What happens when the subject ingests lighter fluid and then forced to swallow hot coals. Test

*subject did, in fact, burn from the inside out.
Fed to pigs*

Is it possible to actually stretch a subject to death? Test subject Heather has been stretched even more. No fight left in her and has been chosen for mummification.

Acupuncture using long hot needles – slowly add burning candles to needles. Test subject Jill has 24 needles inserted into her now; three in each breast, arm and leg. Candles placed on the needles and lit.   Test subject no longer responsive to rape.

Make a small incision in gut to pull out the intestines. Restrain subject for animals to munch on. Test subject succumbed to experiment. Fed to pigs.

Suspend subject above bamboo shoots and wait for them to grow into the subject. Test subject Maria has been chosen for this torture. Bamboo is growing into the body. Discomfort noticed.

***

Sheriff Hamilton knew the package would be from David Thorguson, there was no doubt in her mind. "Alex, I received another package."

If Alex knew when poor Jordan would receive a package, he would commandeer it before she even saw it. He was worried about her and her pregnancy. She was so close to her due date that the stress couldn't be good for her. "I can take it right to the task force office, if you'd rather Jordan. That way you don't have to worry with it."

"I can handle it; I just don't want to be the one who opens it."

Inside the carefully wrapped package was a human tongue with a note "I'm having way too much fun to stop". Alex also noted that the package was shipped from West Virginia once again. David Thorguson and his accomplice had found a hunting ground.

Chapter 35

Dear God, please let me die. I'm ready to die, to end this suffering. She had been dreaming she was back at home, in her bed. If only she could go back to that dream. She would rather be anywhere but here.

Jill kept imagining herself on a beach, a tropical island far away from here, from him - no them. She attempted to escape reality, but the pain prevented her mind from wandering off. She tried to picture someone else, anyone else but this monster, raping her. She no longer cared what he did to her body; she had been degraded and defiled in front of her friends for days now. She had lost track of how long she had been here. With each savage thrust, his fury with her increased. She no longer screamed or fought back. She just lay there, motionless. This angered him more and she knew it. Maybe he would finally end her suffering.

He slapped her across the face hard. "Please stop. I can't take it anymore."

"Your pleas do nothing for me. You deserve this; you are nothing but a whore. I am in control of you; I can force you to do whatever I want."

The rape seemed to last forever. Her insides were on fire. She was raw from his brutality.

Chapter 36

Hannah was having a bad day today. Very seldom did she feel sorry for herself and let the depression of being diagnosed with MS take over.

She should be excited. Her new line of Multiple Sclerosis, MS jewelry was complete. She had been working on this for quite a while now. The line had to be perfect. All profits would go to the MS Society, to help with research. Maybe one day there would be a cure for this disease, or at least a better understanding of what the disease did to your body.

This was one of those days where depression moved in and refused to let go. She couldn't wait to see Frank later today. His support had been amazing. He is the best thing that had come into her life in a very long time.

When her ex-husband left her because of the MS, Hannah assumed her life was over. Somehow, she managed to pick herself up from the ruins and channeled her energy into her growing business. Now Doug, her ex, was sorry he left her. It didn't help that the whole town thought he was an ass for what he did. He had tried on several occasions to "win" her back. She had learned her lesson. Her life was better without him in it. Doug never believed her "jewelry" would ever bring in any money. He constantly told her it was a complete waste of time and money; that she should find a new hobby. Well, she managed to get the final laugh. Karma could be a bitch, when she chose to be.

As soon as Frank saw her he could tell that she wasn't feeling well and put his arms around her, holding her tightly. She knew that he wished he could take her pain away and make her feel better.

He kissed her gently, holding her close to his body. She didn't resist, needing his closeness. She slid her arms around his neck, pulling his mouth closer to hers. The kiss deepened. For a brief moment in time, she wanted to forget about the MS, the depression and the pain associated with it. Her blood began to heat with desire. Frank picked her up and carried her off to the bedroom, both falling onto the bed.

His hands found their way under her dress and pulled it over her head in one swift movement. She worked on the fly of his jeans, anxious to feel him against her skin. She felt his warm breath against her breast, kissing one nipple while massaging the other. As he teased and nipped ever so gently, the nipple hardened in response. She arched against him as desire warmed her to the very core.

"You are so beautiful, Hannah, don't you forget it." As he rolled on top of her, she welcomed the weight of him. Her body responded to his kisses trailing down her body. The stubble of his beard tickled the inside of her thighs, as he slipped his tongue inside her, igniting a fire deep within. She arched upward as his tongue delved deeper into her womanhood.

"Frank. I love you so much." She wanted to show him the same pleasure that he was showing her. She pushed him down onto the bed this time. As she straddled him, she trailed kisses down his body. He was already hard, throbbing for her.

"Hannah, if you don't stop right now, I'm not going to be able to hold back."

"What's wrong, Sheriff, can't take the heat?" As quick as lightning, he was back on top of her, thrusting himself into her, filling her up completely. She felt the first waves of orgasms wash over her and they kept coming.

***

Sheriff Ourso listened to Hannah sleep as he thought about the case. It had him stumped. He had talked with Steve and his friends, but no one seemed to know why someone was taunting them. Adele Fisher and the others were still missing with no leads. He was beyond frustrated and he had a feeling Steve and his friends were holding out on him. He knew it deep down in his gut. There was more to this story than they were telling him. The problem was, how in the hell could he find out? Ourso had to tread carefully. These were some prominent and powerful people he was questioning. Maybe Hannah knew what they were hiding. She grew up with them.

Chapter 37

The Traveler remembered how much Chloe Hatfield hated spiders. One day during class, a spider was on her desk and she actually became hysterical. It took a while to get everything ready for her, but now that it was complete, he was anxious to see what happened.

The life-size aquarium was unbreakable. The plexiglass cost more than he expected. It ate up a good bit of the money he made from selling pigs. He hoped it was worth the cost. The spiders were easy to obtain. There were more than enough around the old barn, and it didn't take long to fill up the aquarium.

The Traveler looked around at his captives. He immensely enjoyed the perverse pleasure he received from the persecution and torture of his prisoners. Now they truly understood the hell of being tormented day in and day out. His diabolical plan was working better than he ever dreamed it would.

David was even happy with things. They were both learning a great deal of self-control also. Their captors were slowly dying off. The pigs had taken quite nicely to the taste of fresh blood.

The Traveler had to follow Chloe for several days to find the opportune time to abduct her. She seemed to always have someone around her. The only time she ever seemed to be truly alone was at night. She had always been a social butterfly at school and craved the attention. It didn't seem like she had ever grown out of that need either.

The Traveler lurked in the shadows, hidden by the trees along the side of Chloe's house. He would have to wait for her to open the garage door so he could enter. Unlike the others, Chloe made sure she set her alarm every time she left or came home. He did manage to knock out all the lights around her house so that the outside would be completely dark. This might be his only chance to abduct her. The anticipation sent tingles up and down his body.

***

Chloe Hatfield enjoyed her job as the loan officer at the bank. Not only did she know the financial information and credit history on just about everyone here in town, she could approve or deny whoever she wanted to for a loan, and there was nothing they could do about it. Chloe's dad was the president of the bank and someday she hoped to have that same position. However, he made sure she worked her way up to it, knew the ropes so to speak. He said the only way to really know the business was to work in the trenches.

Chloe woke up to the feeling of being tickled. As she became fully awake, she realized it wasn't a tickling sensation as much as something crawling up and down her skin.

She was paralyzed with fear. This had to be a nightmare. How in the world did she end up being covered in spiders? She tried desperately to push herself free. The glass cage surrounding her refused to budge. She tried hitting the glass with all her might and couldn't seem to break it.

She was too afraid to scream. She didn't want the damn spiders to crawl into her mouth.

***

The Traveler enjoyed watching the show. However, David wasn't too pleased, he would rather torture her himself. He would make it up to David and take him hunting in another neighboring town.

He wondered how long it would take for little miss sunshine to scare herself to death, or die from all the spider bites. The Traveler wasn't sure which spiders were considered poisonous. He wasn't even sure if he had a poisonous spider in there. For all he knew, they could all be poisonous. From the way she was thrashing around in there, he would say they were more than likely sinking their fangs into her flesh at this very moment.

Macabre Torture Journal

Mummification – while the subject is alive. Test subject Heather had been chosen for this.

Immense pleasure received from watching brains bleed from the nose. Fed to pigs.

Length of time it takes for rat poison to kill the subject. Test subject Barbara is being submitted to this torture. Poison increased – more discomfort noticed.

Does phantom pain truly exist – removal of a limb from subject. Test subject Adele had her left leg amputated just below knee.   Complains of left foot pain.

Confine subject in glass coffin full of spiders – Test subject Chloe was chosen for this experiment. Extreme discomfort noticed right away.

Acupuncture using long hot needles – slowly add burning candles to needles. Test subject Jill has 30 needles inserted into her; five in each breast, arm and leg. Candles placed on the needles and lit. Test subject Jill no longer responsive to rape.

Suspend subject above bamboo shoots and wait for them to grow into the subject. Test subject Maria has been chosen for this torture. Bamboo is growing into the body. Extreme discomfort noted.

***

Milburn Hatfield arrived at the bank at his usual time and expected to see Chloe already at her desk. He was proud of his daughter and he had a feeling she would be ready to step into his shoes in no time. She could be a real hard ass when it came to loaning out money, which had kept foreclosures and repossessions down greatly, even in this economy.

When Mr. Hatfield peeked into her office, he saw that she hadn't made it in yet. He jotted down a quick note for her to stop by and see him whenever she had a chance. He planned on taking her out to lunch, to catch up and find out if she had heard anything from her friends. She had been upset over these disappearances. Milburn checked on Dylan Robinson, Sr. yesterday and he looked as if he had aged ten years since Dylan Jr.'s disappearance. Everyone in town seemed to be second guessing Frank Ourso as sheriff since he had no leads in the case.

By lunchtime, Mr. Hatfield still hadn't heard from Chloe and decided to give her a call to see if she wanted to go out to lunch. Her office phone just rang, so he tried her cell, which went straight to voicemail. Maybe she was in with a customer and too busy to answer her phone. He would go ahead and walk down the hall and ask. That way, they could leave together. When he arrived at her office, she wasn't there. After asking around, no one seemed to have seen her all day. Now he was worried, especially with all of her friends disappearing.

He made a call, "Sheriff Ourso, its Milburn Hatfield. No one has seen Chloe all day and she isn't answering any of her phones. I'm getting ready to head over to her house."

"I'll meet you there. Please wait for me before you go into the house."

Millburn Hatfield didn't want to wait for Sheriff Ourso, but agreed nonetheless. He didn't know if he could handle finding anything disturbing in her house. He prayed everything was alright.

Sheriff Ourso pulled up right before Milburn Hatfield. "Do you have a key to her house?"

"Yes, I do."

"Wait here." When Chloe didn't answer the doorbell or his insistent knocking, Sheriff Ourso let himself into her house. "Miss Hatfield, its Sheriff Ourso. Your dad is worried about you and asked that I come by."

There was no answer. The house was extremely quiet. Minutes later, Sheriff Ourso walked back outside to find Milburn Hatfield pacing back and forth. "I'm sorry, sir, but she isn't inside. Would you mind looking around to see if you notice anything missing?"

Mr. Hatfield walked around, but the only thing he could find strange was that the pantry seemed to be completely devoid of food. "Except for the fact that Chloe needs to go grocery shopping, nothing seems to be missing."

***

Sheriff Hamilton knew from the size of the package the delivery driver was bringing in, that it was likely to be another human organ. There was no way her stomach could handle it. This time the package was addressed to Alex. Maybe David Thorguson was finally giving up his fascination with her.

"Alex, the package was addressed to you this time. It's fairly large."

Now Alex was curious. Why was David Thorguson sending him packages instead of Jordan? What could be inside, and why the sudden change?

Jordan wasn't sure if she even wanted to look inside, "I think I'll give you some privacy. I'm going to go get me something to drink."

Alex carefully opened the package. Inside was a human brain with a note, "Dear Alex, I decided to send you a brain to study. I know how the human mind fascinates you."

The package was shipped from West Virginia again. Alex called Agent O'Riordan to check in, "I received a package from West Virginia today. It contained a human brain."

"David Thorguson sent you the package this time?"

"He did. It looks as if he is still hunting in West Virginia."

"I've been watching VICAP carefully and asking law enforcement agencies there about any murders. So far, nothing fitting our duo's MO has been noticed. Do you think they changed their MO?"

"No, I believe they have found a hunting ground that they are comfortable with. This time, they do not want the bodies to be found."

Chapter 38

The Traveler remembered his senior year well. After a long hard summer of working on the farm, he had managed to develop quite a muscular body. Gone, was the lanky teen from his junior year. He just knew his senior year would be special. He couldn't wait to ask Emily Harris out.

One day after school, he built up the nerve to ask her. He waited for her at her house. His palms grew sweaty just thinking of her. He had even bought a small bouquet of flowers, so she would know how special she was to him. He would make her forget all about her boyfriend.

He was so nervous, he had a hard time talking. He couldn't believe it, the bitch laughed at him. "Did you honestly think I would actually go out with someone like you?"

The Traveler was heartbroken. The next day at school, everyone knew he had asked Emily Harris out on a date. The teasing became worse. He was the laughing stock of the school. He would never forgive Emily Harris.

***

Emily Harris Stanford was finally on her way home. Where had her life gone wrong? She had been so popular in high school, cheer captain, prom queen, and even married her high school sweetheart. Now, she was all alone and working a dead end job. In retrospect, she should have paid more attention to the nerds instead of the jocks in school. Maybe then she would have had a happier life. She should have listened to her parents and went to college, instead of getting married. At least she would have an education to fall back on.

Her kids were entering their teenage years and reminded her so much of herself growing up. Maybe they would learn from her mistakes. She could only hope.

The heels of her shoes clicked on the sidewalk, echoing through the night. Thankfully, she was almost to her car. She enjoyed her new hostess job at Harmony but hated working two jobs to make ends meet. At night, all she wanted to do was fall into bed.

Fog and a pitch-black night made visibility almost impossible. A light rain was falling and even the moon and stars were hidden. A chill swept across her body. She swore she heard footsteps coming up behind her. She stopped to listen; nothing but silence. She was being silly and needed to get a grip on her overactive imagination. Suddenly, an electrical shock traveled through her body.

Emily was slow to wake up. Excruciating pain tore through her body. Her head felt like it was about to split wide open. She was lying on her stomach, with her arms and legs tied together behind her. The restraints were too tight; she couldn't seem to pull herself free.

Cautiously, she took in her surroundings.

It looked like she could be in a barn, but she wasn't sure. Terror started to swallow her whole. She had a hard time breathing.   Why on earth had someone brought her here?

Once again, she tried to break free. She must escape. There had to be a way out of this mess. She needed to get hold of herself.

When Emily saw her captor, the color drained from her face. Every now and then your past really did have a tendency to catch up with you.

* * *

The Traveler couldn't wait to torture Emily. "I've dreamed about this moment for oh so long. Don't worry, I'm not going to kill you right away. Where would the fun be in that? My friend has a special torture picked out for you, but first, I want to have some time with you."

David anxiously waited to see if he could cut out a living heart. All of his other attempts had failed in the past. It had been difficult to get to the heart and his victims died too quick. He managed to find a pair of tree pruners that should cut through the rib cage. Now, to see if it would work while she remained awake.

The Traveler slipped his hands around Emily's neck. He felt her heartbeat drum against his thumb. The shock from the Taser had worn off. She struggled against the restraints. He could see the desperation and fear in her eyes.

A malevolent smirk formed on his face. "There is no chance of escape. You can scream all you want, there is no one to save you - or hear you for that matter. All your friends can do is watch in horror, as we seek our revenge against you."

A sob rose from her throat. "Please, I'm sorry. I just want to go home."

"I'll show you the same mercy that you and your friends showed me." He felt her pulse quicken.

She wrenched harder against the restraints as he squeezed a little harder around her neck. A moan escaped from her lips, causing him to increase the pressure around her neck.

He savored the rush of power flowing through his body, knowing he controlled her fate in his hands. He let up and allowed her to gulp in as much air as possible, before tightening his grip around her neck once more.

He felt her heartbeat lessen, missing a beat every now and then. Her lungs burned, craving air. He loosened his grip, allowing her to gasp for air once again. "It's time for you to rest, Emily. Soon, my friend will want his turn with you."

Macabre Torture Journal

Length of time it takes for rat poison to kill the subject. Test subject Barbara was being submitted to this torture.   Poison increased – more discomfort noticed.

How long does it take a heart to stop beating after removal from a live subject? Test subject Emily was chosen for this experiment. Unfortunately, the heart beat only mere seconds after removal from the body. Fed to pigs.

Does phantom pain truly exist – removal of a limb from subject. Test subject Adele had her left leg amputated just below knee. Subject is constantly in pain. Bleary eyed.

Confine subject in a glass coffin full of spiders – Test subject Chloe was chosen for this experiment. Extreme discomfort noticed right away.

Acupuncture using long hot needles – slowly add burning candles to needles. Test subject Jill has 30 needles inserted into her; five in each breast, arm and leg. Candles placed on the needles and lit. Test subject Jill no longer responsive to rape.

Suspend subject above bamboo shoots and wait for them to grow into the subject. Test subject Maria has been chosen for this torture. Bamboo is growing into the body. Extreme discomfort noticed.

***

Emily's kids made it home from their dad's later than they were supposed to on Sunday. Evan was concerned that their mom wasn't home, but his sister, Erica, told him he was being silly. "Man Evan, get a grip. Mom probably found herself a man. You can be such a worry wart."

The next morning even Erica was worried, "Dad, mom never came home last night and she wasn't here when we got back to the house yesterday." Their dad wasn't that concerned, and told them if she didn't show up by the time they came home from school, to give him another call.

Erica and Evan both had practice after school, so it was well after dark by the time they arrived home. Their mom still wasn't there, but she might be working the night shift. They decided to wait until the morning. After leaving a quick note as to where they would be, they took off to their dad's to wait for her to return.

As much as Tom Stanford loved having his kids home with him, it had been several days and they still had not heard from Emily. Even though he had a lot of problems with Emily in the past, she had always been a good mother to her kids and he knew she wouldn't go this long without seeing them. If he was five minutes late in bringing them back home, she was usually up his ass about it.

After dropping the kids off at school, he headed over to the Sheriff's Department. He asked the receptionist up front, "Who do I need to talk to about reporting a missing person?"

"Let me get Sheriff Ourso. He will want to talk to you."

Sheriff Ourso came up front to meet Tom Stanford. "Sir, who did you want to report missing?"

"My ex-wife. When I took the kids back on Sunday afternoon, she wasn't home. They assumed she was at work already, pulling an early shift. When they woke up the next morning, she wasn't home, but figured she was still at work. She sometimes works overtime, trying to earn as much money as she can." He didn't harp on the fact that his ex-wife could never have enough money, which was one of the things they fought about.

"The kids called me worried, so I picked up them up and left a note for her, so she wouldn't freak out when she saw that the kids weren't home. After several days, I knew she wasn't working or off having a good time somewhere. Even though Emily has her faults, she loves the kids and wouldn't abandon them. Those two are her whole life."

Sheriff Ourso could eliminate the ex-husband as a suspect in the woman's disappearance, if he had the kids and was reporting her as missing. This meant he had another missing person. "Sir, do you know if she was friends with Michael and Jill Redmond, Dylan Robinson, and Barbara Swanson?"

"Yeah, we were all in the same clique in high school and she has stayed friends with them ever since. I have kind of been kicked out of the clique since our divorce, but I stay in touch with Randy Jenkins whenever I can. Why?"

"I'm not sure if you have heard, but they are all missing, along with some of your other friends. Randy Jenkins is among those. I would like to send a detective to her house and check everything out."

"Of course, whatever you need."

The last time Emily had been seen was after work, walking to her car. It turned out her car had been impounded as an abandoned vehicle. The car was being processed, but so far nothing had turned up.

Chapter 39

The putrid odor of death roused her from her unconsciousness. The stench was so potent that it caused her to gag. She tried to take small, shallow breaths to keep from breathing in the foul odor. The unrelenting pain cut through her like a knife. Every inch of her hurt, throbbing and burning. Her insides were on fire from the savageness of the rape. Fear and nausea started to overrule her senses. If she had anything in her stomach she knew she would vomit. Maybe an empty stomach was something she should be thankful for.   She tried to get control of the fear rising up inside of her.

The darkness that seemed to constantly surround her started to diminish, daybreak must be at hand.   She tried to think of anything, other than the overwhelming stench and pain. If only she was back home, or anywhere other than here. She had lost track of time, she could no longer remember how many days she had been here. If she could escape, she could send help for her friends.

She noticed she had been moved. As her vision improved, she noticed her arms were chained to a beam in an old barn. She felt something slithering around her feet. A shudder of fear crept down her back, she was standing in a pile of snakes. They were slithering around her feet; some coiling as if to strike.

She tried to pull harder on the chains, she had to free herself. Maybe she could somehow lift her feet out of this barrel of snakes, or at least stand on the edge of the barrel.

When she lifted herself up, trying to get her legs away from the snakes, she heard wood splintering. Maybe, just maybe, the wood was weak enough to break loose. She was glad now of all those extra workouts at the gym. She pulled herself up one more time. More splinters fell on her head.   This may be her only means of escape. Her muscles started to weaken from the exertion; her body was damp from sweat. She never considered herself a quitter, ever, but she began to lose her resolve.

People had to be looking for them by now. Someone had to have noticed that they were missing and informed the cops. Any day now, they would be rescued from this hell hole. What kind of crazy bastard would do this to another human being? She didn't know anyone this deranged.

A menacing chuckle snaked through the air, "Are you afraid yet?"

She refused to let him know how terrified she actually was, "I am not afraid. People know we are missing and they will come looking for us."

"They will never find you. They probably don't even care that you are no longer around. How many others have you been cruel to? Does anyone really care about you, or are they glad you have all started to disappear? If anyone does find you, it will be too late. Your friends are already starting to die. You can smell their rotting flesh, even as we speak."

***

A feeling of satisfaction swept through him as he realized his plans, his very dream, was coming to fruition. All those that had tormented him were almost all here. Some had already died at his hand, but others were still being tortured. Only a few remained to be brought to his prison.

Chapter 40

An intense pain roared through Rose McKey's head. Whatever drug her captor had used, left her with the worst hangover she had ever experienced. She always heard the warnings about never leaving your drink unattended, but she never took heed to it. Something like that never happened around here.

Her eyes were finally adjusting to the darkness. The moonlight offered a soft glow to the room. It looked like she was being held in an old barn of some kind.

Before she could think of a plan of attack, her captor appeared before her.

"What are you planning on doing to me?"

He laughed at her menacingly. "You mean that you don't recognize me after all these years?" Rose McKey had always used her beauty to get whatever she wanted in life. He would be the one to take that beauty away from her. Not only would they use the acid to see if her eye color changed, but he planned to use it on her face to take away her beauty. He wanted to bring her down a peg or two. Life could be so harsh at times.

She stared hard at him. He looked vaguely familiar, but his eyes were blank, vacant, as if he had no soul. Then she noticed the knife in his hands. He ran the knife along her body, letting it caress her neck, arms, the swell of her breasts, moving downward.

"Please, let me go, I promise I won't tell anyone."

"Oh, but my friend and I aren't ready to let you go. We haven't even begun to have fun with you."

Panic sent shivers down her body, "Friend, what friend? You mean there are two of you?" Out of the shadows stepped another man. She knew she was doomed now. She watched as the other man picked up a knife, light glinting off of the steel.

***

He felt her body tense and smiled to himself. He could see the fear building in her eyes. Her breathing picked up, causing his erection to become rock hard, almost throbbing with intensity. Her voice grew shaky as she begged him. "Please, don't hurt me!"

He looked down at her. She reminded him of a deer caught in the headlights. He would enjoy playing with this one. She looked as if she was ready to pass out from fright itself. It wouldn't take long to break this one and have her screaming in agony.

Their screams were such sweet music to his ears. The smell of blood teased his senses. He traced her stomach with the tip of the knife. He brought the tip to the cleavage between her breasts. White hot pain scorched through her body, stealing her breath away, as the knife slipped into her tender flesh once again. Warm blood oozed down her body.

Her brown eyes began to lose their vitality. Soon, she would die and one more would succumb to his revenge.

They could no longer torment him. The sun was starting to rise. Sunlight slowly filtered its way into the barn. The carnage would be revealed in the daylight.

Chapter 41

The disappearances had people on edge. No one had heard from any of those that had disappeared. Something or someone had caused their demise, he just couldn't prove it. Even with patrols stepped up day and night, they had found no clues as to what was happening around here.

Hannah had stepped over to the Sheriff's Office to see Frank for a little bit. While he was on the phone, she checked out the local wanted posters the FBI always faxed over to the police stations. One in particular caught her attention. That was the guy she had seen at the hardware store, she was positive. The other man looked so familiar; she just couldn't put a name to the face. She hated this side effect of MS; her memory just wasn't as it used to be. People she went to school with and had been around her whole life, over half of them, she couldn't remember their name or all of the good times they had. She wished at times her life was back to the way it used to be as far as that part was concerned. There was so much she just didn't remember anymore and she worried it would only get worse.

She heard Frank hang up the phone. "Frank, come see. This was the man leaving the hardware store. I wish I could place the other man that was with him, but for the life of me, I can't."

"Hannah, are you certain this is the man you saw?"

"I'm positive."

"That's not good news at all then. But, that may also fit, since you said you saw a motor home. This is an escaped serial killer down in Hope, Louisiana. It is believed that another potential serial killer helped him escape. I need to get on the phone with this Agent O'Riordan and find out more details, just in case." He gave her a quick kiss.

Hannah knew from talking with Frank his mind was turning. She continued to stare at the picture. His eyes seemed almost lifeless.

Frank called the FBI hotline. "My name is Sheriff Frank Ourso, in Lake Hamilton, West Virginia. We may have a sighting of one of your most wanted, David Thorguson. The motor home was also seen. "

It didn't take long for Agent O'Riordan to get on the line. "Where did you say you are located?"

"Lake Hamilton, West Virginia. Listen, we haven't found any bodies, but we have had several prominent citizens disappear. They just vanished into thin air. I did have a sighting of a motor home, but there is a national park not far from here, so it's not unusual for motor homes to be seen in the area."

"We have reason to believe these two hide out in parks to torture and kill their victims. Is the park large enough where they could be hiding the bodies there?"

"Yes, it is and there are quite a number of various walking trails, and a fairly large lake."

"This is the first big tip that we've had. Would it be possible for you to send me what files you do have on the missing persons, so that I can review those? I and a few others are going to head that way, if you don't mind?"

"You are more than welcome to come into town. I plan on taking a ride out to the park to see if a motor home is parked there."

"Sheriff, I know it goes without saying, but please be careful. These men are very dangerous."

Sheriff Ourso decided it would be best to go in pairs and check out the park. No motor homes were at the park and the manager had not had a motor home fitting that description stay there. That wasn't to say that one hadn't been there during the day. Where the hell was that motor home then? Hannah wasn't the only one that had mentioned seeing it.

Agent O'Riordan received the email with attachments from Sheriff Ourso. With several prominent people disappearing, they may be on the right track. Once they were in the air, he informed the task force about the most recent developments. "I know we usually have a meeting before taking off, but time is of the essence. Several prominent people in the town have disappeared without a trace. No bodies have turned up either. Sheriff Ourso and a SWAT team already checked out the local park but found no motor home. A search and rescue team had already searched the area when a couple went missing from there a couple of weeks ago, but nothing turned up from that search. A second search and rescue team is being sent out to the park, this time with cadaver dogs. I believe that our duo has found another area to hide. The park is popular and we do know from past experience they like quiet places."

By the time Agent O'Riordan and the task force landed, search and rescue had been working the area for several hours. Sheriff Ourso met them in the parking lot, "Thank you for coming. So far we haven't had any other leads. The search and rescue team hasn't had any luck. The cadaver dogs haven't found any bodies either."

Chapter 42

Daylight came rushing into the old barn. Their tormentor stood in the middle of the room, with a self-righteous look on his face, emitting a crazed cackle. His eyes glowed with hatred. "Welcome to my own personal hell for all of you. This is still better than any of you deserve. Especially after everything you put me through." He was actually gloating.

"I've been planning this for a long time now. My friend here has helped everything come along nicely, don't you think?" They could hear the satisfaction in his voice. Now, they all had to wonder, or worry, if they somehow created this monster. They'd bullied plenty of kids, even grown adults, over the years and none had turned into a raving psychotic maniac. That was until now.

***

Taking a long, hard gulp of the whiskey, Stephen felt the burn settle deep into his gut. If only the alcohol could take away the pain and guilt consuming his body. Looking over at Adele's side of the bed, he swiped away a tear as the grief and loneliness once again overwhelmed him.

As he drowned his sorrows away, the phone rang. When he saw the time, he cringed. This was the call he had dreaded since her disappearance.

Anxiety filled him as he found the courage to answer the phone, "Hello."

In a maniacal voice The Traveler responded, "Do you miss her?"

The despair ignited into confusion, then an all-consuming anger when he realized it was the man who had abducted the love of his life, "Where is she, you son of a bitch?"

Shaking his head, "Now, is that the way you should treat the man who has your wife?"

Biting back a hateful comment, he asked, "What do want? Where is she? Is she okay?"

With a smirk, The Traveler motioned for David to move closer to Adele. "I thought perhaps you would like to hear your wife accept your punishment."

The Traveler held the phone out for Stephen to listen while his wife was repeatedly tortured.

"Did you hear what you have done? You did this to her."

With each anguished scream, it felt like a knife had pierced straight through Stephen's heart. His voice quivered as he began to plead with the man, "Please, let her go, take me instead. I'm begging you to stop."

"No! You did this to her. I want her blood on your hands. When you close your eyes, you will hear her screams. You will never find peace, just like I never received any peace from you."

When she let out an animalistic scream of pain, out of pure instinct, he stood to defend her and then fell to his knees with tears pouring down his face. Through the haze, a sound caught his attention. Something about the sound triggered a memory.

Bolting to his feet, he immediately called the one man who could help him. "Sir, I know who has them."

"Come get whatever you need, just bring him back to me."

"Yes sir, and, sir, thank you."

"You better be right about this, son."

After Stephen hung up, he began making plans to get their loved ones back. For this to work, he would need help. At least Mr. Robinson had a gun collection that every man here was envious of.

Chapter 43

Jeremy and Kelly Thompson had just returned from their cruise. It had been a great vacation and neither wanted to return home. Kelly's parents agreed to watch the kids, so they could have some time together. Jeremy had never gotten used to being a member of a close knit family. Hell, he hadn't spoken to his brother in over a decade. Once he turned eighteen, he left and never came back. When their parents died, Jeremy wasn't able to locate him. He knew his brother wouldn't come home for their funeral. His parents were never loving, affectionate parents. Jeremy had a hard time shedding a tear for their deaths.

Jeremy hadn't even gone back home to check on the old house or camp. The properties were probably decrepit by now. With the market the way it was, the property wouldn't even sell. One of these days, he would face his demons and go back home.

There was a stack of mail and newspapers on the counter. Cheryl, his mother-in-law, had a nice meal waiting for them and she was anxious to hear all about their vacation. "Jeremy, I put an article on top of the newspapers that you might be interested in reading first. The little town you grew up in has made the news. Several prominent members of the town have gone missing. There is also an article and even a sketch of the person they believe is a serial killer the

FBI is searching for. If I didn't know better, I would say it's you. There are an awful lot of similarities in your appearance and the one in the sketch."

He remembered how his brother always talked about how much he hated the "elite" in town. They always seemed to bully him and teased him relentlessly. His brother wouldn't be involved, though. He swore he would never step foot in that town again. Jeremy picked up the sketch and looked at it. Sure enough, he would swear that was his brother. He couldn't believe it; there was no way his own brother could be a suspected serial killer.

Jeremy went into his office and closed the door. He decided it would be best if his family didn't hear this conversation. He wasn't even sure if he should be making this phone call. However, if Lance was involved, then Jeremy didn't want him looking up Jeremy or his family. Jeremy's life was perfect right now and he didn't want any problems. His own wife didn't know much about Jeremy's childhood and he wanted to keep it that way. She didn't need to know he grew up in poverty and how bad his childhood was.

Dread came over him as he dialed the number. "This is Jeremy Thompson, may I please speak with Agent O'Riordan. I believe I know the identity of the man in the sketch. The one he is looking for."

"Hold on one moment, please. " Ellen couldn't believe her ears. The article had run a while back and they hadn't had any good tips come in. "Agent O'Riordan, there is a Jeremy Thompson on the line. He says he knows who the man in the sketch is. I know we usually look into the tips before calling you, but he is from West Virginia, sir."

"This is Agent O'Riordan. How can I help you, sir?"

"Agent, I won't beat around the bush. I believe the man in the photo may be my brother, Lance Thompson. I haven't seen him in years, so I can't say for sure, but there is a family resemblance. My own mother-in-law thought it was my picture. My family owns a house and an old pig farm in Lake Hamilton, West Virginia. That's where we grew up."

This may indeed be the break they needed. He wrote down the addresses of both locations. They would need to send a SWAT team to each address. Since Jeremy was part owner of the properties, he gave permission for the search.

Agent O'Riordan informed Sheriff Ourso, "It looks like things may be falling into place. I received an ID on the man in the sketch. I even have the go ahead to search the property where the perps may be hiding out at. I can get the task force up and at your office in no time. Do you think you can line up SWAT again?"

"I will give them a call right now."

Agent O'Riordan repeated the information that Jeremy Thompson had given him and said, "Let's get everything moving. Do you know the area well?"

"I do. The pig farm is located in a woody area, lots of places for the perps to hide. We need to go in as silent as possible. It may even help to have air support, in case they take off on foot. Not that we have a good chance of catching them if they do escape. Lance grew up in those woods and he will know every hiding place there is. Going in silent is our best chance. I don't think they are at the house. The neighborhood isn't a busy one, but a motor home would have been noticed. A pig farm may explain why no bodies have turned up. We can only hope that we are able to locate the bodies, if there are any. We also need to go in during daylight hours. This is one place we don't want to go at night."

"The task force is on their way. I'll make a call to see about air support. I'll have everything I need to do on my end ready for 1:00 p.m."

"That sounds good. We don't have to worry about evacuating anyone out there either. My team and I will meet you out there. Agent O'Riordan, please express to everyone the importance of going in silent. Noise echoes out there and we don't want to give them an advantage."

***

Josh Robinson felt uneasy about what they were planning. "Stephen, are you positive about doing this? Maybe we should have gone to the sheriff?"

Stephen cocked his gun and glared at Josh, "If we had gone to the sheriff, he would have waited until he had enough evidence to request a search warrant. Well, I don't want to wait! I want my wife back now, alive." Stephen looked over at the men, "Does everyone remember the plan?"

Everyone nodded in agreement and swallowed back their fear. Even from here, they could smell the death and hear the strangled moans that filled the still air. Pure, unadulterated rage consumed Stephen at just the thought of everything his wife must have endured.

***

By 12:50 p.m., everyone was there, suited up and ready. The Kevlar vests felt heavy in the heat of the day. Air support would give them a two minute head start, as to not scare them off with the sound of choppers approaching. With guns drawn, Agent O'Riordan gave the signal to move in. As they approached the farm through the woods, they heard the muffled cries. Sheriff Ourso and Agent O'Riordan looked at each other. The cries could only mean that there was someone here and they were indeed still alive. Agent O'Riordan gripped his Glock a little tighter and moved forward cautiously, searching for any sudden movement. He heard another distorted moan. There had to be more than one person in there. As they moved closer to the barn, he could also make out talking. His adrenaline kicked in. Sheriff Ourso moved into his line of vision and held up two fingers and pointed to the door.

They inched to the doorway, guns drawn. "FBI!" As if on cue, SWAT moved in from the rear of the barn. FBI agents, SWAT, and deputies charged in with guns drawn. Nobody was prepared for what they saw.

Sheriff Ourso went pale as a ghost. "Holy Mary, Mother of God." Everywhere you looked, there was carnage. Several men and women were shackled in makeshift cells, and others were restrained to inhumane torture devices. Even with all his years of experience, Agent O'Riordan had never seen anything like this.

A man was strapped to a chair, writhing in pain. A naked woman, with streaks of blood running down her body and eyes hollowed out from obvious signs of malnourishment, knelt over him screaming, "Now, how do you like that, you bastard." She had somehow managed to stab him in the groin with the same knife he had tortured her with. Looking into her tear-filled eyes, he could only imagine the horror she had been through.

Besides the knife in the groin, the group had repeated some of the same tortures on him as they had been forced to endure.

The glint of the gun barrel caught Sheriff Ourso's attention. "Son, drop the gun. Let us take over. They will not get away."

Stephen shook his head "He has to pay for what he did. At least let me kill him first." Sheriff Ourso felt the hate emitting from Stephen.

O'Riordan recognized the desperation in this man's eyes. They had to do something quick, most of the survivors were near death. Placing his hand on the barrel of the gun, he pointed it down, "Son, he is near death. I promise you, he won't live much longer."

O'Riordan pointed at Lance Thompson's restrained body to reaffirm his comment. An involuntary shudder racked through his body at the sight in front of him. This group of individuals had sought out their own justice. He was too near death for saving. Perhaps if they had moved in an hour sooner.

It took a moment for the situation to register in his mind, "Wait a minute. Where is David Thorguson?" Looking Stephen directly in the eyes, he asked, "What happened to the other man with Lance?"

Stephen looked at O'Riordan with a dumbfounded expression, "There was only one man here."

Son of a bitch! Agent O'Riordan got on the phone. "We need to get paramedics in here now. Forensics can move in, but let the coroner know he will need a van."

The next call was one call he dreaded making, "Alex, David isn't here. We are searching the area now, but so far there have been no signs of him."

Adele pushed away the water Stephen tried to give her and rasped out "He…He…He…said that he had a need…" Taking a breath in, Adele tried to finish her sentence, but O'Riordan feared he knew what she was going to say.

"Alex, he is headed your way."

O'Riordan knelt down to the injured woman, "Do you know how long ago he left here?"

In a weak voice, she responded, "Lost track of time. At least one morning ."

O'Riordan hollered out, "Someone figure out how long it takes to get from here to Hope, Louisiana."

As dusk fell over the heavily overgrown property, the forensics team was still gathering evidence. They found the wood chipper the men used to help dispose of the bodies. It looked as if the bodies were dropped right in and the chute dumped the remains directly into the hog trough. Agent O'Riordan wasn't sure if he would ever be able to eat pork again. There was no telling how many bodies were disposed of here.

***

Jordan looked at her watch and grimaced. It was only two o'clock in the afternoon and she was ready to call it a day. On top of everything else, she could not get comfortable. As she walked out the door, she informed Detective Johnson, "I'm going to call it a day. Call me if anything happens."

He looked at her and saw just how pale her face was. "Sheriff, you don't look so good. Why don't you let me drive you home?"

Before she could answer, a pain gripped low in her back. She was ready for this baby to make its entrance into the world, and give the inside of her body a break. Shaking her head, "No. I'm okay. Just tired. Besides, Alex will be home soon."

They had found a house they agreed on. Alex was overseeing the movers at the new house, and she didn't want to disturb him. With the mood she was in this afternoon, she would rather have a few hours to herself. Let him deal with the headache of moving. As she buckled the seat belt, a sharp pain gripped her stomach. For a moment, she considered calling Alex, but decided a warm bath may help ease her aching muscles.

If this was labor, then she still had a while to go before it was time to go to the hospital. She would rather pass away the time at her home than in a hospital bed.

***

After trying Jordan's cell phone with no luck, Alex called the Sheriff's Office, "Please tell me that Jordan is there."

"No sir. She told Detective Johnson that she was going home. She looked tired when she left here."

Damn it. The realization that Jordan may at this very moment be held by a sadistic serial killer scared the shit out of him. He instructed the dispatcher, "Send an ambulance, SWAT, and whatever else you have to my house. I think David Thorguson is headed there."

As he drove home, Detective Johnson called, "I tried to reach her on the radio and her cell phone with no luck. It just rang and rang."

"I know, I can't reach her either. Jordan wouldn't ignore a phone call."

"She wasn't feeling good. Maybe she fell asleep."

Even after Detective Johnson spoke the words of encouragement, neither man truly believed them. Detective Johnson kept blaming himself. He should have insisted on driving her home.

Alex pushed the car to its limits, as he rushed home. He prayed that he arrived in time. Cold fear constricted Alex's heart, as visions of the victims flashed through his mind.

***

As Jordan dropped her keys on the entryway table, she heard a noise in the kitchen. She was surprised that Alex was at home. She didn't recall seeing his car out front. "I'm surprised you are home already. I thought for sure you would wait until the movers were done."

When she walked into the kitchen, the blood in her veins turned to ice.

"Did you miss me, *cher*? As much as I enjoyed playing with my new partner, I couldn't stop thinking of you. You are all I thought about when I took a woman. No one else would do, I had to have you. I couldn't wait any longer."

Jordan inched her hand up to her holster as she listened to him talk. Fear started to take over and she pushed it aside. She drew in a deep breath as another sharp contraction hit her. Now was not the time for her to go into labor. She had to focus on protecting herself and her unborn child.

A smirk formed on his face and his features turned cruel and harsh. His voice became deadly, as he aimed a gun right at her bulging stomach. "You know you should be very afraid of me. I have never played with a pregnant woman before and right now my mind is full of ideas."

Jordan bristled, "You should also know that I will not allow you to harm my unborn child." As she talked, she slowly withdrew the gun.

Before he could react, she aimed her gun at him. "It appears we are both armed now."

Another sharp pain seared through her lower stomach as a hard contraction hit her. The intense pain caused her to stumble, but she managed to keep her balance. David saw this as his chance and lunged at her with the knife he wielded in his other hand. His only mission was to injure her enough to subdue her.

Jordan reacted out of instinct alone, and fired her gun. A stunned David fell, and landed hard on top of her. Her hand moved to her left side, as white hot pain tore through her body. Warm blood began to flow between her fingers at an alarming rate. She felt her body go limp, as she slipped into darkness.

Both Detective Johnson and Alex had made it to the house at the same time, when they heard a shot ring out. Alex kicked open the door, and felt his world come to an end when he saw Jordan crumpled on the floor.

Voices began to talk all around her at once. Dark shadows moved in as hazy images appeared. Her brain tried to process what was happening.

Jordan's last conscious thought was how she would never see her baby's face. Time stopped as a peaceful silence enveloped her.

Detective Johnson made sure that David was restrained before rolling his body off of Sheriff Hamilton. He didn't want to take any chances where this man was concerned. Alex called for the First Responders waiting outside "Get the medics in here now. She has lost a lot of blood."

Detective Johnson kneeled down by David Thorguson and checked for a pulse. "It was a kill shot. He's gone."

Alex squeezed Jordan's hand and called out to her, "Jordan, I need you to hold on, sweetheart. The medics are here."

Jordan heard someone calling out to her. In a weak voice, she said, "The baby…"

The First Responder gently moved Alex out of the way, "Sir, you have to let us work."

Alex moved out of the paramedics' way, so they could tend to her injuries. One was busy taking her vitals as the other started her on fluids. The medic informed his partner, "We have to go. The baby's heart rate has dropped drastically. Call the hospital and let them know we have a pregnant police officer coding. It appears that the knife entered the womb."

Alex felt the ground underneath him open up. If only he had arrived sooner. The ride to the hospital seemed like an eternity. He didn't know what he would do if he lost her. He picked up one of her hands and squeezed it, "Jordan, hold on. I can't lose you or our baby. Think of your family, and how excited they are about the baby. We all love you."

Before Alex could wrap his mind around what was happening, they had arrived at the hospital. Everything was all a blur as her body was draped and wheeled into the operating room.

Detective Johnson patted his shoulder firmly, "She is in good hands. Just think, it won't be long now before you can meet your baby. Soon, we will find out if you have a son or daughter."

Alex watched the operating room doors as he waited to hear what was happening with Jordan. His stomach was in knots as he thought about what all could go wrong.

Alex couldn't get the picture of Jordan's pale face and the puddle of blood around her out of his mind. He had never been this scared before.   He could not get over how life could change in the blink of an eye. Just when he had found love, it could be snatched from him.

He didn't know what he would do without Jordan. He loved her and their unborn child, more than life itself.

As soon as the nurse walked into the waiting room, he worried that the news wasn't good. The beep of the heart monitor echoed in the hospital room. The shuffle of feet beyond the room, muffled voices, and the clatter of rolling carts went unnoticed by him. Alex couldn't move from this spot, as he stared at the small figure lying in the bassinet next to her mother.

Jordan looked so small and frail in the hospital bed. He despised seeing all the IV's and tubes that were going into her body. He tucked the blanket around her small frame, needing to touch her.

Jordan heard someone calling her name, "Jordan...Jordan...Come on, honey. Open your eyes for me just once, my love."

Another voice, a female voice, was talking, "The doctor prescribed her something for the pain. It should help her feel better soon."

Jordan cleared her throat and tried to speak. Alex stood above her with worry etched on his face. He gently squeezed her hand.

She barely whispered, "The baby?"

Alex smiled as he told her, "We have a beautiful little girl. She is perfect. She has the blackest hair I have ever seen. The biggest eyes and sweetest face you could ever imagine. She looks so much like you; it is unbelievable."

Alex placed the baby into the anxiously awaiting arms of her proud mom. Jordan smiled down at her child with tears in her eyes. This may not be how they envisioned their baby coming into this world, but she would be very well loved.